THE BEAT

Sudden Death

A horrible thought occurred to Dean. Joe knew where he lived and was hanging out with Darren. Suppose there had been a break-in at Mary's, as Neil thought? Suppose Joe and Darren were behind it, behind Mary's death, too?

No, that was too awful an idea. Joe wouldn't try to steal Dean's stuff. But, next time they met (there would always be a next time) Dean would ask Joe about what he was doing there. It was no way to treat a friend, but Dean had to lay down the law.

Visit David Belbin's homepage at
http://www.geocities.com/SoHo/Lofts/5155

POINT CRIME

THE BEAT

Sudden Death

David Belbin

SCHOLASTIC

Scholastic Children's Books
Commonwealth House, 1–19 New Oxford Street,
London WC1A 1NU, UK
a division of Scholastic Ltd
London ~ New York ~ Toronto ~ Sydney ~ Auckland

First published in the UK by Scholastic Ltd, 1997

Copyright © David Belbin, 1997

ISBN 0 590 19396 1

Typeset by TW Typesetting, Midsomer Norton, Somerset

Printed by Cox & Wyman Ltd, Reading, Berks

10 9 8 7 6 5 4 3 2

All rights reserved

The right of David Belbin to be identified as the author
of this work has been asserted by him in accordance with the
Copyright, Designs and Patents Act, 1988.

This book is sold subject to the condition that it shall not,
by way of trade or otherwise, be lent, resold, hired out, or
otherwise circulated without the publisher's prior consent
in any form of binding or cover other than that in which it
is published and without a similar condition, including this
condition, being imposed upon the subsequent purchaser.

This one's for Carol and Rob

The city in these pages is real. The events described in them are not. All of the characters, together with the police station where some of them work, are imaginary. The author wishes to thank the many people, including serving police officers, who helped him with this series. He alone is responsible for any mistakes.

PROLOGUE

Mary Brown turned on Radio Nottingham for the football, then hobbled upstairs to collect the dirty laundry. Dean, her lodger, got through clothes like nobody's business. In the kitchen below, a radio commentator read out the Forest team list. Dean, Mary heard, was in the starting line up for the first time. The goal he scored against Spurs must have decided the manager. She was sorry not to be at the game, but her arthritis had been playing her up and Dean insisted that she take it easy. He was a considerate lad.

Mary was at the top of the stairs, with her arms full of sheets, when she heard the sound of breaking glass. She froze on the spot. On the radio, Sheffield Wednesday kicked off.

"I thought you said there'd be nobody in," an

angry voice complained.

"They'll have left the radio on to make it look like they're home."

"What if the old lady…?"

"She always goes to the matches, according to Dean."

How did they know what Dean said? Mary felt a bad twinge in her leg as she tried to decide what to do. The laundry was heavy. She shouldn't be carrying bulky things, not at her age.

"Hey, look at this football!"

"Come on," the first voice said. "Upstairs."

Mary didn't have time to get to the phone in her bedroom. Where could she hide? Rapid footsteps were coming. Maybe if she locked herself in the … but her leg had gone to sleep. There was no way for her to escape.

"You get the hi-fi. I'll carry the TV and video," the second voice said. "If we're lucky he'll have… What the—?"

The youth had got halfway up the stairs before spotting Mary, and now stopped. Mary tried to summon up an authoritative voice, to say "Get out of my house" or something like that. But the sound which came from her mouth was more like the bleating of a lamb being led to slaughter.

"Let's get out," the first one said.

"What for?" the other, bigger one asked from the stairs. "She's seen us now."

"Listen, missus," the first one said, "we're friends of Dean's, all right? We came here to play a practical joke on him. Course, we didn't know you'd be in. We're going now."

"Like hell we are," the other one said, and advanced up the stairs.

Mary, still rooted to the spot, did the only thing she could think of. She threw the dirty laundry at him. Sheets and shirts and boxer shorts tumbled through the air, covering the youth. But he kept coming, looking like a comic-book ghost, his foot slipping on a pillow case as he reached the top of the stairs and fell against Mary.

Mary reached out, trying to regain her balance, but the youth was trying to hold on to her, too. They were both falling, a young man and an old woman tangled together in a sprawl of sheets and limbs. Mary felt every stair as they clattered to the bottom, expecting each moment that one of her bones would break. The sheets cushioned her, but only until she cracked her head against the Minton tiles on her hall floor.

Her eyes were closed when the boy pulled the sheets off her. The last thing Mary heard before passing out was a string of swear words from the lad as he got to his feet.

"You've done it now," the other one said, as Mary sank into an unconsciousness from which she would never return. "You've killed her!"

1

County were playing away, so Neil had opted to do football duty. He needed the overtime. It felt good to be back in uniform for a change. Also, he wanted to see Nottingham Forest's multi-million-pound summer signing in action. Umberto Capricio was an Italian international, a prodigious goal scorer and, with his long brown curls, a bit of a heartthrob, too. Attendances were well up since his arrival, but the team still languished in the lower reaches of the Premier League. That seemed to be their lot in life these days: either fighting relegation, or chasing promotion from the division below. Still, they were doing a lot better than Neil's team, Notts County, who were stuck in the Third Division and had recently lost to Forest at home in a Coca-Cola cup first leg.

This afternoon, another player impressed Neil: a local lad called Dean Sutherland. He'd come on as a sub in the last two games, nearly scoring in both. Forest had bought him from Mansfield Town for two hundred thousand pounds, a bargain if ever there was one. Already, ten minutes into the game, Dean had had a chance saved by the Wednesday keeper. As Neil watched, the lad laid on a beautiful pass for Capricio to blast over the bar. He was a natural.

The game as a whole was no classic. The Wednesday defence soon learnt to close the youngster down and he took a knock shortly before half-time. Neil wasn't surprised to see him substituted after the interval. The game ended nil-nil.

There was no trouble after the match. Neil went back to the station and changed. Then he went to meet Melanie, his girlfriend, in the Bell, one of three pubs in Nottingham which claimed to be the oldest in the country.

"Guess what?" she said.

"What?"

"I've found a flat."

Neil's heart sank. Melanie had been staying with him since returning to Nottingham the weekend before. She'd talked about getting a flat on her own, but Neil had never believed it would happen. What student could afford to live by herself? She'd be far better off staying with him, even if her parents didn't like the idea.

"Where is it?"

"Lenton. A cul-de-sac called Wellington Square."

Neil knew it. Ruth, the girlfriend of his former partner, Ben, used to live there. The street was full of cheap bedsits.

"Lenton. That's a fair way from—"

"Eight minutes by bicycle. I timed it today."

Melanie had brought her bicycle back from Reading with her.

"How much?"

She told him the rent. It was reasonable.

"And Mum and Dad said they'd pay the deposit for me."

Neil was sure they would.

"You've already spoken to them?"

"I had to. There was a queue of people going to see the place. If I hadn't taken it straightaway—"

"*You've already taken it?*"

"I can move in tomorrow. Oh, Neil, you're not going to be upset with me, are you? It's so convenient for the university, and there's no way I could live with you for the next two years, is there?"

She must have seen the disappointment in his eyes, because the next thing she said was, "I mean, neither of us is ready for that yet, are we?"

"No," Neil said, not looking her in the eye. "Of course not."

*　　*　　*

As he drove home, Neil told Melanie about the game.

"It was a lot less interesting after Dean Sutherland went off. First half-hour, Dean played a blinder."

Neil didn't know why he bothered. Melanie was even less keen on football than Clare, his ex. But then she surprised him.

"Dean – isn't he that lad who lives on your street?"

"Pardon?"

"Lanky, very blond hair, face set in a permanent grimace."

"That's him."

"He lodges with Mary, four doors down."

"How do you know that?"

Melanie grinned. "I've seen him a couple of times when you were out at work. He tried to chat me up the other day, rather clumsily I must say."

"Blimey."

Neil thought of footballers as gods, not blokes who might live on the same street as him.

Melanie went on. "I wasn't interested, so he started going on about how he was in the Forest First team, how he'd scored for them. Actually, I thought he must be exaggerating. Anyway, I told him 'sorry, but you're not going to score with me'". He only looked about eighteen."

"He is only eighteen."

Anyone but a fooball hero, and Neil might have been jealous. Melanie was very attractive. Other blokes were always trying it on with her.

"He took it in good heart, anyway. Told me he'd still be around when I changed..." She stopped speaking as they turned into Neil's street. "Look. There he is."

Dean Sutherland was running down the middle of the narrow road, tears streaming from his eyes. Neil braked and pulled down the window.

"You've got to help me!" Dean shouted. "It's my landlady. I think she's dead!"

Ben Shipman felt uncomfortable. Ruth, his girl-friend, was showing their holiday snaps to Paul and Clare. They were round at Paul's for a meal, which Clare had cooked. According to Sam, who was Ruth and Clare's landlady, Clare had practically moved in with Paul this last week. She and Inspector Paul Grace were mad about each other.

What made Ben uncomfortable was that Paul Grace was his boss. Not his immediate boss. That was Jan Hunt, a sergeant who was two or three years older than Grace. Ben was comfortable with Jan socially. But Paul Grace was an Inspector. He had real authority and influence over Ben's future in the police force. Clare might no longer be under his command – Grace had arranged her a transfer to CID before she got her toothbrush in his bathroom – but Ben was.

Ben didn't know what Clare saw in Grace. He was quite a small man and hardly handsome, as far as Ben could tell. The Inspector was good at his job, an efficient bureaucrat. However, on tonight's evidence, there wasn't much to him outside work. He didn't have a lot of conversation and barely pretended to be interested in the photos. Which was fine with Ben, who didn't much want to discuss the holiday anyway. As Ruth put the snaps away, he decided to get the Inspector talking about the one thing which interested all four of them: work.

"What's the latest on the motorway team?" he asked.

The motorway team were so-called because they always chose targets within easy reach of the Midlands motorway systems, ensuring a fast getaway. No one knew who they were, or where they were from. But they were very good at what they did, and had chalked up at least nine successful burglaries. To the burglary charges could be added possession of an offensive weapon, kidnap, false imprisonment and some form of assault. Yet, so far, surprisingly, no one had been seriously hurt by them.

The team specialized in raiding the homes of celebrities. The three members of the team would clear the place of easily saleable goods, then take the celebrity, or more likely their spouse, to a cashpoint machine at knifepoint, where they would clear out as much of the victim's bank account as they could manage. A special task force, based in Birmingham, was trying to track the team down. So far, no one had got near them.

Except, maybe, for Paul and Clare. They had caught Gordon Loscoe, the lottery millionaire who claimed to have been burgled by the team. He turned out to be a fraudster, but it had taken some proving. And it looked like Loscoe knew more about the real motorway team than he'd let on.

"It's three weeks since the motorway team did Candia Arnold," Paul told them. Candia Arnold was a supermodel who had been burgled before Ben and Ruth went away. "If they run according to form, they should do another job in a week or two."

"They're incredibly good, aren't they?" Ruth said. "I mean, you almost have to admire them. No one's been badly hurt…"

"Yet," Paul interrupted.

"Well, all right, they certainly threaten violence. But they're professionals, they don't need to use it. And they don't leave clues."

"Is that right?" Ben asked. "The Birmingham task force still have no leads?"

"No good ones," the Inspector said. "Clare and I had an idea or two, but they weren't interested. After all, Clare's only a DC and I'm a uniformed plod."

"What was the idea?" Ben wanted to know.

"That bloke in the Mercedes who you spotted going into the Wilders', remember?"

Ben remembered. "Eddie something," he mumbled.

"That's right," the Inspector said. "Eddie Broom. He isn't one of the burglars, but from things we've overheard, he seems to know a lot about the team. And he was in the area of a lot of the burglaries shortly before they happened."

"So why can't he be one of them?" Ben asked.

"Broom has a perfect alibi for each of the robberies so far. Which is suspicious in itself. No one has that many alibis unless they knew in advance that they were going to need them. I reckon Broom's the key to cracking the case."

"Where does this Broom bloke live?" Ben asked.

Clare answered. "We couldn't find out, not even when he was in for questioning. But we do know one thing – he sleeps over at the Wilders'."

"Who with?" Ruth asked. "Shirley or Julie?"

"Shirley, of course. Broom's forty. Julie's only a kid."

Ben felt relief, followed by a twinge of guilt. Mention of the Wilders made him uneasy. Before going on holiday, he'd been more than a little tempted by the attentions of Julie Wilder. She was, if not quite a kid, still only seventeen. Julie knew he had a girlfriend, but had made a play for him anyway. Ben hadn't done anything about it. But he hadn't told Ruth what had happened, either.

The thing was, even when he and Ruth were away,

Julie Wilder kept cropping up in his imagination. Ben couldn't help it. She was what other coppers would call "a bit of rough" – didn't her mum go out with a crook? But Ben knew better. Julie was intelligent, resourceful and rather beautiful. Beside her, Ruth seemed plain and a bit boring.

Stop this! Ben told himself. *It's a silly obsession.*

Paul Grace was talking. "So keep an eye out when you're on the beat around that way, and if you see or hear anything about him…"

"I'll tell you," Ben promised.

"Enough shop," Paul Grace said, putting his arm around Clare's waist. "Let's go through to the living-room and crack open that bottle of Metaxa you brought back."

Cause of death, the doctor told Neil, was either a fractured skull or a heart attack. Maybe both. Scenes of Crime had found possible signs of a break-in. A glass panel on the back door had been smashed from the outside. But nothing had been taken, at least not that anyone could see. There was no other physical evidence of a burglary. No one on the street had heard anything, not even the glass breaking. So maybe Mary's death was an accident and the broken glass a coincidence. But Neil wasn't keen on coincidences.

"It could be that she was upstairs when someone tried to break in," he told Dean Sutherland, "carrying the sheets and stuff that were at the bottom of the stairs, and tripped as she was coming down to confront them."

"It doesn't look like a break-in to me," Dean said. "There's a phone in her room. She could have called the police from there."

"That would have been sensible," Neil said. "But people don't always do the sensible thing when they're being burgled. They see it as an invasion of their space. They're outraged."

"Mary wasn't like that," Dean said. "She'd have been scared. Anyway, if there was a break-in, what happened to the burglars?"

"They probably saw what happened and panicked, did a runner. Trouble is, without witnesses or evidence, our chances of catching the burglars are virtually nil."

Dean, still in shock, stared at the floor.

"What are you going to do tonight?" Melanie asked him.

"Go back to the house."

"Where someone just died? That doesn't sound great to me. Can't you go back to your family in Mansfield?"

"My mum and dad split up. My dad and I hate each other and I don't get on with Mum's boy-friend. It's not a good idea."

"One of the other players, then?" Melanie suggested.

Dean shook his head sullenly. "I've only been in

the team a few weeks," he said, scowling. "I don't make friends that easily."

Melanie gave Neil a look. He understood what the look meant: *do your duty*.

"I guess you'd better stay here," he told the young player.

"You can have my room," Melanie said. "I never use it anyway."

"That's brilliant," Dean said. "Thanks."

"I've got some packing to do," Melanie went on. "Neil, why don't you take Dean to the pub?"

Neil took the footballer to the Gladstone. If he took Dean to the Grosvenor, some of the young, trendy crowd would be all over him.

"Pint?"

"No, ta," Dean told him. "I've seen what booze does to some players. Never touch the stuff. Orange juice, please."

They propped up the corner by the coat stand, undisturbed by the other customers. They talked about the day's match. Dean told Neil how proud he was to be playing for Forest, how glad he was to be out of Mansfield. Neil asked why.

"The estate I used to live on, half the people I knew were trouble – thieving, drugging it, smashing up people and places. There was sod-all to do, know what I mean? School was crap. The only thing I was any good at was football. But people respect that.

Turn down a drink or a joint because you've got a game, and no one calls you a wimp."

Neil asked more questions, but Dean kept turning the conversation away from himself, so Neil told him a bit about his own life. He'd played football once, but never had the talent to make much of it. He explained how his dad died when he was in his teens and why he'd joined the force. He mentioned meeting Melanie while he was working, saying that she was a burglary victim, without going into the story of the rapist who had been stalking her building.

"She's what I'd call a real perk of the job," Dean said. "Why's she moving out, if you don't mind me asking?"

"It was always a temporary thing," Neil said, embarrassed. "Mel's only nineteen. That's too young to live with someone."

"If you say so," Dean said.

Neil changed the subject. Of course, people who knew that Melanie was staying with him would assume that she'd chucked him, or gone cold on him. Whereas, really, she'd never lived with him, not properly, just used his house as a place to store her stuff during the summer vacation. Neil had hoped for more, but Mel was right: why rush things?

2

"My mate fancies you," Curt Wilder told his sister, Julie, on Sunday morning.

Julie hadn't had a boyfriend for a few weeks now, not since she chucked that loser, Dave. She laughed. "And what would I want with a spotty fifteen-year-old?"

"He's not fifteen. He's older than you. Eighteen, at least. His name's Joe."

"And how do you know this Joe?"

"He lives round here. Has done for a couple of weeks. Me and Nat have been round his house."

"He has his own place, does he?"

"He shares it with a mate."

"And what does he look like?" Julie asked, though she wasn't really interested. The only man she'd fancied since Dave was Ben Shipman, a handsome black police officer who was way out of her league.

"Average, you know."

"He's better than average," Curt's girlfriend, Natalie Loscoe, put in. "Quite thin, longish hair. He's all right. I'd go out with him."

Curt punched her playfully in the ribs. Natalie was Gorden Loscoe's daughter. The two kids had accidentally given Loscoe's game away, not that Natalie cared.

"And does he have a job, this Joe?" Julie asked.

Curt gave her a dismissive look. "Who's got jobs round here?"

It was true. The Maynard Estate had the highest unemployment in the city. A bloke across the road worked as a train driver, but Julie's mum was more typical. She did a few hours' cleaning a week which she didn't declare to the social. It just about kept her head above water.

Curt, not embarrassed to be setting up his sister, asked again. "Will you meet him then?"

Julie thought about it. She wasn't bad-looking, she knew that. She used to get offers all the time, even when she was with someone. But since Tammy came along, meeting blokes had become more difficult. Last night, like most Saturday nights, she'd stayed home, alone. Mum wasn't the sort who'd look after the baby while Julie went out. Mum was only thirty-three. She liked to have a social life herself. Julie got lonely.

"You can bring him round if you like," she told her brother. "I'm not going anywhere."

"Joe's all right," Curt said. "You'll like him. He even knows one of the Forest players."

"Everyone says they know one of the Forest players," Julie told him, then added, jokily, "I'm only interested if it's Umberto Capricio."

Now there was a man. As Curt went upstairs with Natalie, Julie drifted off into a fantasy. Daydreams were the nearest she got to a decent love-life these days.

After dropping Clare off at the cathedral, Paul Grace drove around. This might be one of the last really sunny Sundays before autumn set in, and he wanted to enjoy it. Also, he valued being on his own for a while. The last few weeks with Clare had been a rollercoaster. They were plunging faster and faster, spending more and more time together. It was wonderful, of course. But, at heart, Paul was a solitary person. He needed time to himself and for himself, or Clare might overwhelm him.

Paul drove away from the city, through West Bridgford, past flat fields of dull green, out towards Bingham and Grantham. An old mate from university lived over in Stamford. Maybe he'd drop in on him, give Clive and his wife a surprise. Though it would be an even bigger surprise, Paul decided, if he were to show up with Clare.

After Bingham, the traffic built up. The other cars would be day trippers, or people going for Sunday lunches in country pubs. Which was tempting, actually. Clare had been in too much of a rush for breakfast, so Paul hadn't had a bite to eat. If he stopped somewhere soon, he could give Clive a ring, too, make sure that he was in and this wasn't a bad time to visit.

On a narrow section of road, the vehicle behind was trying to overtake. Paul, in his fast car, wasn't used to being overtaken and anyway this was a stupid place to do it. There were several cars in front of him. The joker behind would never overtake them all. But Paul pulled in tight to the kerb anyway, letting the maroon BMW shoot past as soon as there was a minuscule gap in the traffic. As it did so, Paul glanced over to see what kind of prat took such a risk for so small an advantage. Then he gasped.

The overtaking driver was Eddie Broom.

Eddie tried to get past the Sierra in front of him, but the driver wouldn't pull over as Paul had. Then, two minutes later, Eddie signalled left. Paul tried to decide what to do. He had the number of Eddie's new car and he could pass it on to the Birmingham task force, let the guy go for now. But that would be an end to Paul's role. And Birmingham hadn't shown much interest in Eddie Broom when Nottingham suggested him as a suspect before. Suppose Eddie was casing a potential burglary victim for the motor-way team? He was nowhere near a motorway, but they were only minutes from the A1, which was much the same thing.

Paul signalled left and followed at a distance. Eddie had seen him only once, very briefly, in a casino. There was no way that he would recognize the Inspector through a rear-view mirror. But would he work out that Paul was tailing him?

Eddie didn't have far to go. As he turned in towards the small village of Cropwell Butler, Paul realized where he was heading for, the Martin's Arms in Colston Bassett, which did the best food for miles around. It looked like Paul was going to get his Sunday pub lunch after all.

"There's something we have to tell you," Mum said, when the Coppolas had finished their Sunday roast.

"Is it the business?" Clare asked.

Dad had been having a hard time for years, but he'd always avoided bankruptcy. Until now. The building trade hadn't picked up enough over the summer. Clare had seen this coming.

"Only partly," Mum replied.

Clare looked at her father. There were patches of grey in his black hair. He was overweight and red-faced, having emptied most of a litre bottle of wine over dinner. He seemed tired, defeated even, and said nothing. It was Mum, as usual, who did all the talking.

"We've decided to separate," she said.

Clare was staggered. "*What?*"

"Since … Angelo, we've found it hard to get along. We've tried our best but … we can't live together at the moment."

Mum looked nervously at Clare, seeking sympathy. But Clare felt no compassion, only confusion. How could her parents do this to her?

"But what will you do? Where will you go?"

She addressed the question to Dad, but he only stared into his coffee cup. Mum answered. "I'm staying in the house. It's too big for one, but we couldn't sell it when we tried before and Nick might move back one day. We just don't know."

One day. This was Clare's *father* she was talking about.

"What will you do, Dad? Where will you live?"

Dad cleared his throat. "I've spoken to your Uncle Angelo."

Dad's elder brother, who Clare's brother had been named after, ran his own building business in Bedford.

"He's helping me to wind up the business here."

Meaning that he was paying Dad's debts for him.

"I'm moving to Bedford. I'll work for him."

"But Dad, that's miles and miles away. I'll never see you."

"I'll visit. You'll visit. We'll stay in touch."

The three of them sat in silence for a while. All sorts of dreadful thoughts ran through Clare's mind.

"Are you talking about divorce?" she asked, eventually.

"No," Mum said. "No divorce."

"Isn't there anything, anything you can do to try and … to try…"

Neither of them answered. *You can't split up!* Clare wanted to shout. *It's against your religion!* But after Angelo died, religion had been as little use to them as it had been to her.

"Have you spoken with a priest?" Clare asked.

"Yes," Mum said. "Both of us talked to Father Jude. He tried to be helpful, but…"

"How about marriage guidance … what do they call it? *Relate*."

"Father Jude suggested that. We've been going for nearly a year now. You see, we've thought about this a lot, Clare. It's not a sudden decision."

"Then why didn't you tell me before? Why?"

Mum looked at Dad, who looked at Clare.

"Because we were ashamed, *tesore*. We didn't want to let you down. But we can't go on living like this. It's time to move on."

Clare burst into tears. Mum and Dad both hugged her. Clare felt ashamed. Her parents were splitting up and it had to be her fault. Why hadn't she noticed? She should have been able to do something about it. Why didn't they seem more upset?

Clare needed to talk to both Mum and Dad, but on their own. They weren't her parents in the same way now, not a couple. They were two individuals who had brought up two children, one of whom they had lost, while the other had left home. Clare had never felt more alone in her life.

"How long?" she asked, finally.

"Tomorrow," Dad said. "I'm going to Bedford tomorrow."

There was nothing else to say. After another few minutes, Clare mumbled some excuses and left. In Forest Fields, there was no one home, but Clare didn't mind. She wanted to be with Paul now, to un-burden herself and be comforted. What she didn't want was to be on her own. Paul would come over, pick her up. She dialled his number. It was answered after two rings.

"I'm sorry, I can't take your call right now. If you'd like to leave a message after the tone…"

Clare banged the phone down. *Where was he? Why hadn't he told her that he was going somewhere?* But Paul wasn't her husband, only her lover. She had no claims on him. Right now, though, she needed him desperately. She needed someone to take care of her.

In her bedroom, by the bedside, was a photo of Mum and Dad which Clare had taken when she was twelve. Angelo stood between them, seven years old, his fringe lop-sided, a silly grin on his face. All three looked so happy, as though everything in the world belonged to them. Clare couldn't bear to look at it. She turned the photo face down, then, burying her head in the pillow, tried to pray.

Paul sat in a corner of the pub, watching. Eddie Broom was ten feet away, his back to Paul, with three men of roughly similar age: fortyish. Paul had memorized the face and build of each man. He'd also overheard snatches of their conversation, most of which sounded innocuous. These guys were professionals. They wouldn't discuss their business in any place where they might be overheard.

There had been a couple of telling moments, though. At one point, the fat one, who Paul later figured was the driver, said something about "Gordon", and the other three laughed. Paul took this to be a reference to Gordon Loscoe.

While Eddie was getting a round in, the youngest-looking one, who had some kind of tattoo on his left arm, asked the fat one a question about the type of wheels he was getting. The fourth man, who was balding and (maybe because of this) looked the oldest, interrupted him.

"Later."

He was, Paul decided, if not the boss, the one they most respected. It showed in the group's body language when he was talking. The four never used each others' names, which convinced Paul that he was sitting next to the motorway team. They would have disciplined themselves never to use names in casual conversation. That way, they were less likely to let a name slip accidentally when they were on a job.

Was this a social visit, or were they planning another burglary? When Paul saw them getting ready to go, he paid hurriedly, then went out to the car park. Pity that his motor, a red Mazda, was so conspicuous. He pulled out of the car park, then backed into a driveway a little down the road. If all four men went in one direction, he would follow them all. If not, he would try to keep up with the bald one. Failing that, he would try to tail Eddie's BMW. He'd like to know where Eddie really lived.

As the first of the four cars came by, driven by the bald man, someone banged on Paul's window. An old man in a two-tone shirt shouted angrily at him.

"What are you doing? This is my drive!"

A second car was going past. Were they all going the same way or…?

"Look at me when I'm speaking to you!"

The guy sounded like a retired school teacher. Paul reached into his jeans pocket for his warrant card, but didn't have it on him. There were no more cars. He hadn't been concentrating enough to get the numbers of the two that went past. He should have taken the numbers of all the cars in the car park, he realized. He'd been so excited about following Eddie inside that he hadn't taken such an elementary step. Paul put the car into gear.

"What the…?"

Paul ignored the man and set off in pursuit.

"I'll have the police on you!" the man shouted, but Paul knew he wouldn't, not unless he lied about it, because Paul had done nothing illegal. He thought he could see one of the gang's car, a blue Rover, heading towards Burton Joyce. Paul followed at a distance, wondering where the other car had gone, the one with the bald man inside. Then, on the outskirts of the village, he lost the blue car.

What was going on? Paul slowed down. There were no houses for the car to have pulled into, only farm tracks leading through fields. And why would they…? Paul heaved a sigh of relief. There was Eddie Broom's maroon BMW driving towards him. Paul must have overshot the rendezvous, but he was getting another chance. He slowed down, just in time to see the BMW turn up an unmarked track. Another car was coming now, following Eddie into the turning. These guys were professionals. They had taken the precaution of all coming by a different route.

Paul had to overhear their discussion to find out where they were planning to hit next. But it was far too dangerous to drive after them. He did a U-turn in the road, drove past the track, then parked on the verge a little down the main road. He walked back along the road and turned up the track, pretending that he was after somewhere private to have a pee. In fact, he was looking for cover. There was a hedge to one side of the track and a ditch to the other. He dropped into the ditch. As a result of the long hot summer, the bottom of the ditch was pretty dry, and, provided he ducked, deep enough to conceal him from a car. Paul scrambled along it, trying to make as little noise as possible.

How long had they been at the end of this track? He calculated that it couldn't have been more than five minutes. How long would they need? The ditch began to twist slightly. Ahead of Paul was a small copse. Sure enough, he could see the cars, all four of them parked in a cluster. The four men were standing by the bald guy's Rover, looking at something which he had spread out over the bonnet. A map, maybe, or a diagram. If they turned, they would see Paul. He moved more slowly, ready to fall to his knees at any moment but hoping that he wouldn't ruin his brand new pair of chinos.

Paul snagged his foot on a broken bottle and nearly tumbled over. The younger of the four men, hearing the noise, began to look round. Paul ducked. What would they do if they found him? This team had never hurt anybody, not seriously. But there was always a first time.

Paul heard movement. Were they coming to look? But then he heard car doors opening, engines revving. The meeting was over, already, and he'd learnt nothing. Paul had to get to his Mazda. As soon as the fourth car had gone, he would run back to it, see if he could catch up with one of them. He heard a car go by, then another, then another. As soon as the fourth one went past him, Paul stuck his head up, managed to get a partial plate of a brown Mondeo which must belong either to the fat one or the young one. Better than nothing. Trousers muddied, he got out of the ditch and began to run after the cars, hoping that none of the men would look back.

The brown car had turned left, towards Nottingham. Paul could see the Rover heading right, towards Bingham. He'd better go left himself, as his car was facing that way. Paul ran towards the Mazda, not noticing until he got to it that there was another car parked in front. Two men stepped out. What would they think of him appearing from the track like this, looking like a tramp?

"I can explain," Paul said.

"I hope so," said the uniformed PC, breathalyzer equipment in his hand. "You see, we've had a report that you ran over the foot of a gentleman who lives nearby, not fifteen minutes ago."

"That's not true," Paul said. "I'm in the job, like yourself, and I'm following a suspect. If you can just let me go after them now, I'll explain later."

"Warrant card?"

"I left it at home, but my name's…" The PC was shaking his head.

"Pull the other one, mate. You're under arrest."

3

Melanie's new flat was dusty and dilapidated. The small living-room had a sofa which converted into a bed. There was a kitchenette on a landing, tucked between the bathroom and the stairwell. The house had three flights of stairs, which were a lot to climb with her heavy stuff. But Melanie was thrilled, so Neil told her he liked it.

"It's great," he said.

"Isn't it? I've never had a place of my own before."

"It hasn't got a phone," Neil pointed out.

"There's a box down the road. I'll save money."

"But how'll I keep in touch with you? Let me buy you a mobile."

"No," Melanie said. "I don't want you buying me

anything. And mobiles are much more expensive to run than ordinary phones. Don't worry. We'll manage."

Was she withdrawing from him? Neil wondered. But if he had learnt one thing from his relationship with Clare, it was to play things cool.

"I expect you want some time to yourself now," he said. "Sort the place out."

"Yes."

"So do you want to cycle over for a meal tonight?"

"No. Lorraine's back in Nottingham today. I said I'd meet up with her. How about you come over after work tomorrow and I cook you a meal?"

"I'd like that."

He drove back to his house, the day spreading out emptily ahead of him. Probably he should go and visit his mum, cheer her up, but he wasn't in the mood. Last time he phoned, Mum kept moaning about his sixteen-year-old sister's new boyfriend and Neil didn't want to get involved. Though Gill would be impressed when he told her that he'd had Dean Sutherland staying at his house. She was a Forest fan. But not a fanatic. Gill took to supporting Forest because her older brother was a County fan and she liked to niggle him.

To Neil's surprise, Dean was still there when he got home.

"I wanted to ask you something," the footballer said.

"What?"

"I spoke to the boss" – by which he meant the Forest manager, in the same way that Neil would mean his Detective Inspector – "and he was sympathetic, told me to stay in a hotel for the night and he'd get me somewhere on the approved list tomorrow. But the approved list is full of old biddies like Mary – they look after you well, but theirs are boring places to live. Thing is, the club doesn't like really young players living on their own or with other players. That's why they have an approved list."

Neil waited for Dean to get to the point. He knew what it was and he wasn't sure what he thought about it.

"Then I mentioned to the boss that I'd spent the night in the spare room at a policeman's house and asked how he felt about that. And he asked how old you were. I said late twenties."

Neil frowned. He was only twenty-three.

"The boss said that he couldn't see me getting into too much trouble if I lodged with you but he'd have to meet you himself, first. So I was wondering…"

Neil didn't know what to say. He could use some extra money. He would get to meet the Forest manager, and the other players, probably. It was an exciting prospect. But he didn't really want to share his house with anyone other than Melanie. Especially not an eighteen-year-old.

"If you let me have the spare room, I wouldn't be any trouble. I was paying Mary…" He mentioned a sum that would more than cover Neil's mortgage. Neil could feel his mind changing.

"But I could afford more."

"No," Neil said. "If I let you stay, that'd be fine, but I'd expect you to sort out your own food and washing. I don't even know how much time I'll be spending here now that Melanie's got her flat in Lenton."

"You don't have to tell the boss that," Dean said, with a smile.

"No," Neil said. "I don't."

"So, what do you reckon?"

Neil would be seeing less of Melanie once term started – she had lots of studying to do. Maybe the company would be good for him. The money certainly would be. And Neil had never been any good at saying No. Still, he hesitated.

"If your boss agrees," he said, eventually, "we'll give it a trial, for a month. Fair enough?"

"Fair enough."

They shook hands on it.

By the time Paul extricated himself from the county coppers who'd stopped him, it was too late to keep tabs on any of the four cars. He drove home and changed his clothes. There were no messages on his machine. Paul badly wanted to see Clare, to talk over what he'd seen. But she was having a family day, and he had to respect that. Anyway, families bored him, and he had no intention of meeting her parents if he could avoid it. He spent as little time as he could with his own.

Paul was a workaholic. There were always reports to be read, paperwork he could do. But today, his mind was entirely on the motorway team. He scoured the Sunday papers. Maybe a journalist would have come up with a scrap of new information, or even a lead. The special task force in Solihull didn't seem to be getting anywhere.

Neil Foster, Paul remembered, had had a theory about the team. He'd thought that they were based in Nottingham. Admittedly, his idea arose from the Loscoe case, which turned out to be a fraud. A question remained: why hadn't the team done anyone in Nottingham yet? They'd done jobs near most other major Midland cities. There were at least two possible answers: either the gang were based near Nottingham, and avoided working where they were known, or they were planning a job in the county, and that was why they'd met at the pub earlier today.

Paul rang the station and got them to do a PNC check on Eddie Broom's car, the only one he'd got a full licence-plate number for. While waiting, he considered what to do next. He needed to talk it over with someone – Clare was the obvious choice, but she wasn't available. His opposite number at CID, John Greasby, might be interested, but he might also think Paul was poaching on his territory. Then there was Neil Foster, who used to be in Paul's shift. But he was Clare's ex. Paul couldn't see the two of them discussing a case socially, not in the near future, anyway.

The phone rang. Eddie Broom's BMW was registered to a company called Chemiclean, based in Spondon, which wasn't far away. Was Eddie living over Derby way, or was Chemiclean a cover of some sort? Paul considered driving over there, but the place was bound to be closed. He would have to wait until tomorrow to find out.

The phone rang again. It was Clare. She sounded upset.

"Thank God you're in," she said. "Can you come over? I need to see you. Now."

"This is Joe," Curt announced.

He was nothing special, Julie could tell at a glance.

"Hi," she said. "I'm Julie."

"I know, I've seen you around the estate, with your baby in the pram."

"That's Tammy. She's asleep at the moment."

There was an awkward pause.

"Joe knows Dean Sutherland," Curt said. "We might get to meet him."

"Who's Dean Sutherland?" Julie asked.

"He joined Forest this season," Joe explained, "from Mansfield Town. He scored a goal yesterday."

"Oh," Julie said, "right. Curt's the big football fan, not me. I like Capricio, though." She added, "So how do you know this Dean, then?"

"We used to live on the same street, went to school together, everything. He's my best mate."

"You must be dead proud of him," Julie said, encouragingly.

"Dead proud, yeah."

There was some friction there, Julie gathered. Jealousy, frustration, whatever.

"So is it him you share a house with?" she asked.

"No. Another mate. Darren. He's from Mansfield, too."

"And where do you live?"

He told her.

"That's a squat, isn't it?"

"Yeah. It's just temporary. I'm looking for something better."

Julie knew the place, a hangout for druggies and worse. Bad things had happened there.

"I might even be getting a place with Dean," Joe said. Then he turned to Curt. "But don't mention that to Darren."

"I won't." Curt went to the loo.

Joe was another loser, Julie could see straight-away. She was getting an eye for them. She felt sorry for him, but not sorry enough to go out with him.

"I thought you might like to come out for a drink later on," Joe said. "Just you and me. What do you say?"

"I've got Tammy to look after," Julie explained, adding, "I'm pretty tired. Another time, maybe?"

"Sure. Would you like to meet Dean? He could get us into a match if you like."

"I'm not that bothered about football," Julie said. It wasn't quite true. She followed Forest, had been to matches with Curt.

Uncomfortably, Joe stood up. He half-smiled. "Nice to meet you," he said. "Catch you later."

"Later."

When Curt came back, Joe was gone.

"You blew him out, didn't you?" he accused his sister.

"I don't fancy him."

"I thought looks weren't all that mattered. You didn't give him a chance."

"Not much of one," Julie agreed. "There was no point in leading him on."

"He's promised to introduce me to Dean Sutherland," Curt said proudly.

"Dream on," his sister told him.

Sam came home before Paul arrived.

"What on earth's the matter with you?" Clare's

landlady asked. "You look like you've been crying your eyes out."

Clare explained about her parents. Sam gave her a hug.

"You poor lamb. That's a rotten thing to happen."

"I feel – I don't know – guilty, somehow, as though I ought to have been able to prevent it."

"That's an understandable reaction," Sam said, "but it's also rubbish. Children might keep a couple together, but I've never known a case where they've caused them to split up."

"Do you think you'd have stayed with your husband if you'd had children?" Clare asked. Sam had been married at twenty, divorced at twenty-five.

"Selfish sod didn't want children. That was a big difference between us. But at least your mum and dad waited until you'd left home before splitting up. Mine didn't."

Clare hadn't realized that Sam's parents were divorced, too.

"How old were you?"

"Sixteen. They waited until I'd finished my exams before telling me that Dad was moving out. Thank you very much. As if I hadn't already noticed that he didn't come home three nights a week. But you don't want to hear abut that now. Look, here comes Paul. Maybe he can cheer you up."

*　　*　　*

"What is it?" Paul wanted to know, immediately. "What's upset you?"

She told him.

"I keep asking myself why," Clare finished. "They always seemed so happy together. Of course, there've been problems with the business, and Angelo dying put an awful strain on them, but they've been through so much together. Mum had to defy her whole family to marry Dad in the first place. I can't believe that they're splitting up now. We're Roman Catholics!"

"It sounds like they've been under a lot of strain," Paul told her. "It's very common for couples to separate after a child dies. They might love one another, and try to stay together, but seeing each other all the time can't help but remind them of the tragedy. The only way to get on with life is to start again on their own. Does that make sense?"

"It makes sense," Clare said, "but it doesn't help. I miss Angelo, too. Seeing Mum and Dad always makes me think of him. But Angelo wasn't their only child. They still have me. What about me? I need them too!"

Paul held her.

"They'll still be there for you," he said. "And remember, you've got me now. I'm here for you. I love you."

It was the first time he'd said those words. Clare

looked into his eyes and knew that he meant them.

"I love you, too," she said.

4

Dean was still in bed when Neil went to work in the morning. His training session didn't start until ten. In the CID room, Neil felt like announcing to the squad that a member of the Forest First team had moved in with him. But such an announcement would also mean explaining that Melanie had moved out, so he decided to leave it for a while.

Clare arrived late, which was unusual. She looked stressed.

"Anything wrong?" Neil asked.

"I'll tell you another time. I need to ring Solihull."

That was where the task force investigating the motorway team was based.

"Why?" Neil asked. "Has Phil Church been on to you?"

Church was the Birmingham liaison. Clare was his Nottingham counterpart.

"No," she said. "Eddie Broom's back. He was seen with some other blokes who might be connected."

"Seen by who?"

No reply. From the look on Clare's face, Neil knew that she meant Paul Grace, her new boyfriend. Did she expect Neil to be jealous? As it happened, he was. Which was silly, because he didn't carry a torch for Clare any more. His feelings must be a hangover from the two years he spent going out with her. He listened to Clare talking after she got through on the phone.

"I think we've got a lead on the motorway team. Four men were spotted in a pub yesterday. One of them was Eddie Broom. I need you to check out a place called *Chemiclean*. It's…" Clare stopped, then listened, then her voice rose until, finally, frustrated, she gave up. "All right, *fine*! You hand it over to the Derbyshire force and they'll sit on it because the council cut their budget again and, in the meantime, the team are about to do another job and all the bad publicity will land on your head, not mine!" She hung up and looked at Neil in despair.

"I haven't had a very good weekend," she said.

"Want to take a drive over to Derbyshire, check

out this place where Eddie Broom might be working?" Neil suggested.

"Why not?" Clare managed a smile. "I could do with getting out of the city for a while."

In the car, Clare didn't mention what was on her mind. Neil didn't press her, but he couldn't keep quiet himself. He found himself telling Clare that Melanie was moving into a place of her own and he had a new lodger.

"He's a footballer. Plays for Forest."

"I thought you supported County."

"I do. But this lad used to live down the street and his landlady popped her clogs at the weekend. Sudden death."

"Accidental?"

"Probably. But there was a possible break-in, so we're investigating. Anyway, Dean's a really talented player. Seems like a nice bloke, too."

"That's exciting for you," Clare said, absent-mindedly. Then she seemed to wake up. "How does Melanie feel about you having another bloke in the house?"

"I haven't told her yet. We're not in each other's pocket."

Clare frowned. "There's nothing wrong with closeness, with involving each other in your decisions, is there?"

"No, I didn't meant that, I…"

There was something she wasn't telling him, but he left it for now. They were turning into Spondon.

"There's the factory, over there."

Chemiclean, a brochure in reception informed them, specialized in a revolutionary dry-cleaning process. They asked to see the manager.

"Yes," he told them, "we have reps working up and down the country. Our system's really taking off."

"Is this man one of your reps?" Neil asked, showing him a recent photo of Eddie Broom.

"I don't believe so. There were a couple of blokes taken on when I was out of the country, though. He might be one of them. What's his name?"

"He wouldn't be using his real name," Neil told him. "Thing is, he's driving a car that's registered to this firm."

"That can't be right," the manager told them. "Our reps all work on a franchise basis. They own their own cars. The only car that's registered to the firm is mine."

"It's not a BMW, by any chance?" Clare asked.

"No, a Sierra. We aren't that successful yet. You say this bloke is pretending to work for me?"

Neil shook his head.

"No. He probably drove by here, wrote down the firm's name and gave it to whoever sold him the car as a fake address. We were following a lead, that's all. Sorry to disturb you."

                        *   *   *

"There's only one way we're going to find Eddie Broom," Clare said, as they drove back to Nottingham.

"What?"

"Watch Shirley Wilder's house. They've had an on-and-off thing for years. He's bound to show up there sooner or later."

"I could call Jan, get her to have her beat coppers keep an eye out," Neil said.

"Paul's already done that."

He would have, Neil thought.

"But that won't be enough," Clare went on. "CID need to watch the house again."

"The boss'll never agree," Neil said. "We're fully stretched as it is."

"I was thinking of evenings."

"The DI would never authorize the overtime."

"But think of the glory," Clare said.

Neil wasn't interested in glory. He preferred to be paid. "Sorry," he told her. "You're on your own."

"Don't I know it," Clare muttered.

"What will you do if you find him? He isn't wanted for anything."

"Yet."

"It's Solihull's job," Neil added, defensively.

"And they don't seem to be doing it very well."

Neil left it there. Back at CID, DI Greasby wanted to know where they'd been. Neil was vague.

"A lead from an old case. Didn't pan out."

"Next time, clear it with me first. Now go and assist Tracey. She thinks she's found a garage that's turning round a lot of nicked cars."

"When's the post mortem result on Mary Jones due?" Neil asked on his way out.

"This afternoon. I'll let you know the result."

Every Monday, Tuesday and Thursday, the Forest players went for a run before their training session at the practice ground in Lady Bay. Dean, not good at getting up, had missed a couple. This Monday, he got to the ground just in time to join in. But he still didn't feel like he belonged. The players ran in friendship groups. Some ran along the high steps and others took the lower steps, right next to the river. Today's was a short run, as far as the suspension bridge, then across it and back along the other side of the Trent.

Dean had only been in the team a few weeks. He hadn't made any firm friends yet. Sometimes he tagged along with a bunch of the younger players. Most days, like today, he ran alone, head down. He listened to the group of tramps gathered by Trent Bridge. Each time any Canada geese approached, they started wagering roll-up cigarettes on whether the birds would fly under or over the bridge. Before he made it as a footballer, Dean used to fear ending up like those tramps.

"Hey, Dean!"

Somebody was running alongside him. It happened occasionally, usually schoolkids skiving off. But Dean recognized this voice.

"Hey, Joe. How you doing? Bit early for you, isn't it?"

"I've got a place near here now."

Inwardly, Dean cursed. The last thing he wanted was Joe watching him train every morning.

"Who with? Whereabouts?"

"It's just temporary," Joe said. "A squat in the Meadows. I'm with Darren. Remember him?"

Dean remembered him all right. An idiot. He used to come to games with Joe. He was in the year below them at school, used to hang out with a real psycho ... what was his name? It came back to him.

"Just him – not his mate Rob?"

"Nah. Rob's still inside, far as I know. Glen Parva. How about you? Still in lodgings?"

"Yeah. That's right."

Dean wasn't going to tell Joe that he'd moved, or where to.

"I was thinking, if you're interested, the two of us might get a flat together."

This knocked Dean off his stride.

"Remember how we used to talk about it," Joe went on, "when we were fifteen?"

"I remember," Dean said. "But that was a long time ago. Thing is, the manager likes us to be with responsible, older people, know what I mean?"

Ahead of Dean, some of the other players were glancing back. Joe, in his scruffy jeans and anorak, looked like he'd been sleeping rough. Dean was embarrassed by his friend.

"Look, mate, I'm falling behind. Stay in touch, all right?"

He put on some speed. Joe, already wheezing, couldn't compete. The last thing Dean heard him say was "There's this girl I want you to meet," but Dean was out of earshot before he heard her name. He felt lousy, letting down an old friend like that. But Joe was his past. The other players were his future.

5

Clare finished work early and visited Mum on the way home. The house was in uproar. A vacuum cleaner was going and the Rolling Stones were on the record player at the same time, each trying to drown the other out. Dad could never stand the Stones. As Clare opened the front door, she noticed the pile of stuff dumped to one side of it. There was Mum and Dad's old bedroom carpet. Not only that, but there was their mattress, too. On top of the pile was the "For Sale" sign which had stood forlornly in front of the house for nearly a year.

As Clare closed the door, the vacuum cleaner stopped. "Nineteenth Nervous Breakdown" came to an end.

"Who's there?" Mum yelled.

"Only me!" Clare yelled back. "You couldn't hear the door bell."

"I'm up here."

Clare followed the sound of her mother's voice into the bedroom which, until yesterday, she'd shared with Clare's father. It was the room where Clare had been knocked out when interrupting a burglar at the beginning of her first day on the beat. It was the room where she and her brother Angelo would come charging in on weekend mornings, waking up their parents with requests to visit the park, or Goosefair, or the Savoy Cinema. It was the room where...

The bedroom was completely empty. Even the curtains were gone. Only bare boards remained. Mum, wearing an ancient pair of dungarees, smiled proudly.

"What *are* you doing?" Clare asked.

"I moved into Angelo's room last night," Mum said. "I only need a single bed now."

"What about when Dad comes to visit?"

"There's your room. Or, if you're staying, the sofa in the front room is reasonably comfortable. I've decided that this is going to be the new living-room. I'm going to sand and varnish the floorboards."

Clare was incredulous. "What have you done with the old double bed?"

"Family First collected it this morning. They'll

pass it on to some family in need. The council are coming for the rest of the rubbish in the morning. I'm giving most of Angelo's stuff to the Oxfam shop. It's in the front room, if there's anything you want."

"I ... I don't know." Clare sat down on the dirty floorboards. She'd expected Mum to be depressed and deflated today. Instead, she was the one who felt that way. Mum sat down next to her.

"You're not upset about me getting rid of Angelo's things, are you? Your father and I did agree that it was time."

"You're right," Clare said. "It's time. It's just... I expected..."

"And I'm not touching your room. So, whenever you want to stay, or if you ever need to move back in for a while, it'll be there."

"I appreciate that," Clare said. "You're not selling, then?"

Mum shook her head. "For what this house would fetch, I'd never get anywhere as nice again. So I decided to change everything around. Guess what? I'm going on a word-processing course, at People's College. I was a secretary before I had you. Remember?"

"Of course I remember." Mum had never officially worked since then, but she had done most of Dad's typing work and accounts for him. "So you're going to look for a job?"

"That's the idea," Mum said. "Or I'll have to take in lodgers. There's not much money coming in. Your uncle Angelo's been generous to Nick, but…"

"I can always let you have…"

Mum shook her head and gave Clare a hug. "I know you would, sweetheart, but I'm going to make it on my own for once."

Clare stared into her mother's beaming face. "I can't get over how *happy* you seem."

"I am happy," Mum told her. "It's a new beginning, for me … and for your father." She looked around her. "New room, new start. You can help me choose some curtains if you like. I was thinking of painting the room a kind of deep yellow. What do you think?"

"Yellow? You're kidding!"

Mum was like a student let loose on the first flat she'd called her own. Clare, confused, tried to play along. "Why not go the whole hog?" she said. "Make it bright orange!"

Training finished early because Forest had a match that night. In between, Dean had a driving lesson. Most of the other players had decent cars and he wanted to be like them. Not that there was anywhere secure to keep a car on the road where he lived. Neil drove a clapped out old Cortina, which no one would want to pinch. Maybe he would let Dean practise in it. But best not to ask yet. Dean didn't want to push his luck.

Joe was waiting in the street when the driving instructor dropped Dean off. Dean groaned. Twice in a day. Joe was with Darren, the headcase.

"Woman who answered the door said you'd moved," Joe commented. "What are you doing here?"

Dean wasn't going to tell them he'd moved in with Neil. The last thing he wanted was these two hanging around when the detective got home.

"Just come to get a couple of things," he said.

It was embarrassing that Joe knew he'd moved before Dean had got round to telling him. With that, and running off this morning, Dean had crossed a bridge, he realized. The friendship was finally over.

"I'm in a bit of a rush actually," he added, wanting to get inside the house. The woman who'd answered the door would be Mary's sister, sorting out her stuff. But Joe and Darren wouldn't know that. Let them think it was his ex-landlady.

"So sorry," he went on. "I can't invite you in."

"That's all right." Joe told him. "We'll wait out here."

"I might be some time," Dean told him, apologetically, then saw the look on Joe's face and realized that he'd just said he was in a hurry. Oh, what the hell, Joe had to get the message. Even Darren could spell it out for him. Dean had no choice but to ring the doorbell.

"So where've you moved to?" Joe asked, but before Dean had to answer, the door opened. Joe and Darren skedaddled around the corner.

"Sorry to disturb you," Dean said to the old woman who answered the door. "I'm Dean. I used to..."

"I know who you are," Brenda said. "Mary told me all about you the last time she rang me. There's a couple of things here which might belong to you. Will you come in?" Dean followed her into the house, which was a jumble of boxes and packing paper. He soon found out that Brenda could talk even more than her older sister. Dean helped Brenda to put away ornaments, photographs, crockery and cutlery as he listened to a potted version of her life history. It was the least he could do. When he finally left, nearly an hour later, Joe and Darren had gone. With luck, Joe wouldn't push trying to find out where he lived now. If he wanted to find him in future, Joe would have to go to the city ground, where it was easy for Dean to avoid anyone he didn't want to see.

But what if Joe and Darren found out his new address? Neil being in the police might put them off, or it might make them all the more eager to embarrass Dean. Joe could still be good company when he was on his own, but Dean didn't like Darren.

The two lads had got together in Glen Parva,

after Dean started playing for Mansfield Town. Leaving them behind – Darren, in particular – had been his biggest reason for getting out of Mansfield. At the end of last season, they kept coming to Town games, chanting Dean's name, even when he was only the substitute. Embarrassing. Joe kept showing up at Mum's house, Darren in tow, wanting to pal up with him like it was the old days and they were still at school together.

Now those days were over and Dean wanted to get on with his new life, if his old friend would let him. Joe wasn't meant to visit him at Mary's. Dean had invented a rule to keep him away. He'd only given him a phone number. When they met, it was in city pubs, but somehow, Joe knew that address. Had he followed him home?

A horrible thought occurred to Dean. Joe knew where he lived and was hanging out with Darren. Suppose there had been a break-in at Mary's, as Neil thought? Suppose Joe and Darren were behind it, behind Mary's death, too?

No, that was too awful an idea. Joe wouldn't try to steal Dean's stuff. But, next time they met (there would always be a next time) Dean would ask Joe about what he was doing there. It was no way to treat a friend, but Dean had to lay down the law.

"Good holiday?"

It was Ben and Gary's first day on the beat together.

"All right."

They continued walking. Ben offered no further details, not even a description of the weather. Of course, Gary had already heard that Ben's holiday was good. He lived in the same house as Ben's girlfriend, Ruth. *Taciturn.* That was the best way to describe Ben, Gary decided. He gave nothing away. But Ben was Gary's mentor. They had to get on.

"Want to hear a joke?" Gary asked. The look on Ben's face indicated that he didn't. They were at the edge of the Maynard Estate, one of the roughest parts of the city. On these streets, many people didn't get up until evening. There was no one to overhear them.

"Which is it better to be?" Gary asked his new partner. "Black, or gay?"

Ben frowned, then seemed to think for a moment. "I give in," he said.

"Black," Gary told him. "At least you don't have to tell your parents."

Ben laughed and Gary relaxed. He'd broken the ice.

"Have you told yours?" Ben asked, as they walked past a boarded-up squat.

"I wouldn't know where to start," Gary replied.

They turned a corner to the street where the Wilders lived. Ben stopped and lowered his voice. "The Inspector asked me to look into something," he told Gary. "I want to go down the back alley.

We've got a reliable informant there – a train driver called Nigel. If Eddie Broom's shown his face again, he might know about it."

The train driver turned out to be a tall black guy. He hadn't seen Eddie Broom.

"How about a maroon BMW?" Ben asked.

"Nope. Just the four of them: Shirley, Julie, Curt and Tammy. Curt has a girlfriend comes round sometimes. That's all."

Ben wrote his home number on a scrap of paper.

"There's an answering machine on that one," he said, "so you can reach me anytime. If you see Eddie, or the car I described, give me a bell, day or night. All right?"

"Sure," Nigel said. "I mean, a BMW, it'd stand out on this estate like a visit from the Queen, know what I mean?"

"He's right," Gary said, five minutes later, when they continued their beat. "Broom would be a fool if he showed up in that car round here."

"He used to come round in his Mercedes," Ben commented.

"But now he knows we're interested in him, maybe he's leaving Shirley alone."

"Maybe. But they go back a long way."

"What a family, eh? I wouldn't like to live on the same street as them."

Ben frowned. "They're not as bad as they're cracked up to be."

Gary raised an eyebrow. He didn't associate Ben with the liberal tendency in the job. Most coppers would call the Wilders the scum of the earth. The (long gone) father had been in and out of prison. The mother went out with crooks and cheated the social. The son, Curt, was one of the biggest petty criminals in Nottingham. And then there was a daughter, who Gary didn't know, but she'd had a kid at sixteen or something like that: following in her mother's footsteps.

Ben Shipman possessed a roving eye. Gary had noticed that. Maybe Ben had a thing for Shirley Wilder. All right, she was a few years older than him and she was a bit of a slapper, but some blokes went for that. And, for the life of him, Gary couldn't see what Ben was doing with Ruth. Gary liked Ruth, but the couple had nothing in common, apart from the police force. And Ruth was, to be blunt, plain, while Ben had the looks of an African prince. He could have whoever he wanted, within reason.

But reason seldom had much to do with people's love-lives.

Before finishing work, Neil rang the doctor who'd done the post mortem on Mary Jones.

"She had a massive heart attack – that's what killed her. Not the fall."

"But which came first?" Neil asked.

"There's no way of telling."

"There may have been a break-in at her house. Were there any signs of a struggle?"

"None at all. Nothing to indicate foul play. But then, there's nothing to indicate the opposite, either. She could have been pushed. Would you like a full copy of the report I'll be submitting to the coroner?"

"Please."

Neil put down the phone. If there'd been any kind of assault on Mary Jones before her heart attack, they were looking at a murder charge – admittedly, one which would be very hard to prove. The only real evidence of a break-in was a broken pane of glass in the back door. Dean said it wasn't done when he left home that morning. But nothing was missing. The broken glass could have been done by kids larking about. Mary would have heard it, hurried downstairs, and fallen. No criminal intent. Accidental death. Except for one thing, Neil thought, as he drove home. The back door was unlocked, which either meant that she'd left it that way, or someone had broken in. Was it usually locked? He would ask Dean tonight.

First, though, he stopped off at Melanie's new flat.

"How was Lorraine?" he asked.

Her friend had been raped in her hall of residence the term before.

"All right, but I don't think she's had a very good

summer. Lots of bad dreams, constant flashbacks. She's having therapy but it's slow going." Melanie sighed. "Tell me about your day," she said.

Neil explained how he and Tracy had kept watch on a garage suspected of dealing in stolen cars, then told her about Mary Jones.

"What's happened to Dean?" Mel asked.

"I was coming to that. I've told him that he can stay in my spare room, on a trial basis, for a month. Is that all right with you?"

"It's got nothing to do with me," Melanie said. "It's your house. But, since you ask, I think the company'll do you good. And maybe we'll get to meet some Forest players. Still want me to cook for you tonight?"

"That'd be great. I'll just go home and get changed."

"Fine. Give me a couple of hours. I'm experimenting with spaghetti."

Neil said nothing, but, inwardly, he groaned. Melanie wasn't much of a cook, and he was bound to compare her pasta with Clare's. Did that make him a fool? He was mad about Melanie, but couldn't stop comparing her to Clare in all sorts of silly ways. He ought to put his ex-girlfriend behind him. But it was hard, when they worked together five days a week. He wondered if she sometimes felt the same way.

6

"You. Me. Paris. The weekend after next."

"That's brilliant!" Clare told Paul, her voice girlish and giggly over the phone. "How do we get there?"

"Plane from East Midlands Airport, then a four-star hotel right by the Eiffel Tower. All paid for out of our casino winnings. Aren't you glad that you're going out with a gambler?"

"No," Clare said, trying to make herself sound stern. She had only gone with him to the casino that one time in order to trap Gordon Loscoe. "I'm not. But I'm willing to forgive you your bad habits when a weekend in Paris is involved."

Someone knocked on his door. "Got to go," Paul said.

* * *

His visitor was Clare's boss, John Greasby, who had finished work for the day. He and Paul were friends, although there were ten years between them. Two years ago, when Paul was the country's youngest sergeant, John had tried to get Paul to move over to CID. Paul stayed in uniform, believing, rightly, that he'd get promoted quicker. Now, here he was, an Inspector, the same rank as John.

"Hear you got arrested yesterday," John teased him.

"I'll bet that story follows me around for years," Paul said, grinning to show that he could take the joke. Yesterday's incident had embarrassed him, and he was still smarting from the indignity of it. "What did the task force make of the information?" he asked. Paul had filed a report first thing this morning.

"That's why I came to see you," Greasby told him. "They didn't."

"*What?* But it's obvious that those men are the motorway team!"

"To you it is. To me it seems pretty clear cut, but DCI Charlton isn't so convinced."

Paul shook his head in disbelief. "What's going on? Doesn't he want to catch them?"

John shrugged. "You know what it's like. They've got endless leads, and everyone would rather pass the buck than risk failure. Until a National Crime

Squad gets established, well-organized gangs like the motorway teams are shooting at an open goal. I tried to get my Chief to authorize me putting a few bodies on it, but … no chance. That's why I've come – to ask you a favour."

"Go ahead," Paul said. "I owe you one." John had taken Clare into his CID squad after she'd started going out with Paul. If she'd stayed in one of the shifts under Paul's command, their relationship would have been untenable.

"I want you and your shift to keep an eye on the Wilder place," John Greasby told him. "Be as discreet as you can. If Eddie Broom shows up…"

"Who do I tell – you or Birmingham?"

"Me. Ideally, we'd have someone on constant surveillance, but…"

"As it happens," Paul said, "I've already had a couple of my boys on the beat checking to see if Broom's been seeing Shirley Wilder again. And there's a house across the road from the Wilders that we can use for surveillance. Got any money in your budget so we can pay the owner something?"

"If you can spare the time, I'll find the cash," John said, getting up to go. "You never know," he added when he was at the door, "there could be glory in it."

"You never know," Paul agreed. A result with the motorway team would certainly extinguish the embarrassment of being arrested.

* * *

Paul rang Nigel, the train driver who lived opposite the Wilders. He was happy to cooperate, even before Paul mentioned money. It never ceased to amaze Paul, the way that some citizens actually *liked* to help the police. Then he rang Clare.

"I'm going to watch the Wilder house tonight," Paul told her. "Will you join me?"

"Can't. I'm going round to see my mum. It's her first night without Dad. I don't know how long I'll be."

"I'll be there from ten until two, just in case you get away early."

"OK, but no promises."

When his shift came to an end, Paul got changed, then took a bus to the train driver's house where he planned to keep watch. His own car was too conspicuous to park in the Maynard Estate, and too likely to be broken into. He let himself in through the back door.

"Notice anything since I rang?" he asked Nigel.

"Curt went out almost as soon as he got back from school. He was wearing a T-shirt which looked ironed, so he was probably going to see his girlfriend. Julie came home at six, wheeling little Tammy in her pram. But I haven't seen Shirley today. Maybe she's at work. Still, I would've thought she'd be home by now."

"Day off?" Paul asked Nigel.

"No. I was on an early. So I'm for bed. You can watch from the front room."

Paul began his dark vigil. When John Greasby asked for help, he hadn't meant him to go this far. But Paul had a hunch, and, since being arrested, he had something to prove.

After the Coventry match, Dean didn't finish signing autographs until well after ten. It had been a tight game, with added pressure because it was being televised live. Coventry had scored early and led for the first hour. Then Dean, who was worried about being taken off, exploited a mistake by a defender to create some space at the edge of the penalty area. He ran round another defender and deceived the goalie by chipping him when he expected Dean to pass. The crowd went wild.

The manager was less pleased, substituting Dean five minutes later.

"Chris had an open goal. You should have passed the ball to him. This is a team game. Any more of that going-for-glory stuff and you'll be back on the substitute's bench for the start of the next match."

The fans queueing for his autograph had no such doubts. Nor did the interviewer from Sky. She asked Dean if he'd heard from the England Under-21 squad manager. Dean, uneasy with the media, fluffed his answer. He was still angry about being substituted, especially as the team had only drawn.

The last girl in the autograph queue was Dean's age and slipped him her phone number.

"I know you've probably got someone, but if not…"

Her name was Karen. She looked fit and Dean nearly asked her out then and there. But he remembered the manager's pre-season warning: *don't chase skirt when you're in the public eye*. The tabloids paid big money for embarrassing stories. He'd give Karen a ring, though. Soon.

Dean was about to call a taxi when a noisy car pulled up alongside him. He looked around to see an old Ford Escort.

"Need a lift?" Joe asked.

"No thanks."

"Come on, Dean," Darren said, in a threatening voice, "get in. Or would you prefer us to run you over?"

Dean looked around. Suddenly, there was nobody about. The supporters had all gone home, or to the pub. There were no other players who he could pretend to be going off with. Reluctantly, he got into the back seat.

"Sorry to come for you at work, but you didn't have time to give us your new address," Joe said, driving over Lady Bay bridge. He didn't look at Dean as he spoke. There was a new distance between them.

"'S all right," Dean said. "There's something I wanted to ask you, anyhow."

"Yeah? What?"

Was that nervousness in Joe's voice? How would he react when Dean asked him if he'd broken into Mary's house? He would deny it. Dean knew that. But he would be able to tell if Joe was lying. He could always tell. Even so, Dean couldn't ask the question outright.

"What were you doing at my old house today?"

"Looking for you, weren't we?"

"I told you not to visit me there. But you did."

Dean couldn't believe it, not really. Joe wouldn't break into his mate's house. But it was Darren who replied. "You told us not to visit because of your landlady, right?"

"Right." As an excuse. Actually, Mary wouldn't have minded visitors. She'd made it clear to Dean that, unless he behaved very badly, she wouldn't grass him up to the boss.

"But your landlady, she had an accident, didn't she? So it didn't matter."

Joe took over, his voice less friendly than ever before. "Reason we were looking for you, Dean, we need a favour. I could put you in a lot of bother, couldn't I? Some of the things you did with me, they wouldn't look good if other people heard about them, would they? So we thought you might do us this little favour, settle the debt, so to speak. What do you say?"

Dean shuddered. This wasn't a friend talking. What did they want from him?

"I'm listening," he said.

7

"Is there someone in there?" Gary asked Ben as they passed a squat on the edge of the Maynard Estate. He pointed at the one upstairs window which wasn't boarded up.

"I didn't see anything," Ben told him.

A sign outside the house said that it was up for sale by auction at the end of the month.

"I definitely saw something moving. Maybe kids use it as a hideout to do drugs."

"Want to take a look?" Ben suggested, without enthusiasm.

"I suppose."

The front door wasn't boarded over, but it had a huge padlock across it. They walked around the house, finding that the boards were loose on a downstairs window. Ben peered into the darkness. They were on the afternoon shift, so weren't carrying torches. Their gear was heavy enough without.

"There's a table underneath the window," Ben informed Gary. "This is their route in and out. You stay here, watch my back."

He climbed in. Gary was already beginning to wish that he hadn't said anything. When it came to small-time drug users, the police were wasting their time. Kids were always going to take drugs and they were always going to find a place to take them in. The ones the police wanted were the dealers, and the people behind them. But Ben was committed now, walking through the darkness. There was a rumble from the floor above. Gary hadn't imagined it. Someone was moving about.

"I'm going up the stairs," Ben called to Gary.

"Wait a moment," Gary called. "I'm coming behind you."

Gary clambered into the house. He was heavier than Ben, and not as fit. His trousers caught on a rough edge of the window frame and he hoped that he hadn't torn his new uniform. There was, he saw, a small patch of light coming down the stairwell. From above, a voice called.

"Who's there?"

"Police," Ben replied, as Gary stumbled after him. "Identify yourselves."

Ben was at the top of the stairs now, Gary at the

bottom. The people upstairs would only get out if they jumped through the window.

"What do you want?"

"You're not in any trouble," Ben replied. "Yet. This is our beat. We just want to know who you are. Show yourselves."

They heard the sound of a door opening.

"There, you've seen me," the voice said. "Now leave us alone."

"I'd like a look around," Ben responded.

"Not without a search warrant."

Gary walked up the stairs behind Ben, so that the squatter could see that there were two of them. Elsewhere on the floor, someone was banging around.

"Prove to me that you're living here," Ben said.

The lad, who was seventeen or eighteen, reached into his jeans pocket and pulled out a brown envelope. He flashed it at Gary and Ben. Gary had time to take in the name, J Hatton, and the address, which was the squat.

"Good enough for you?"

"Do the building society know you're here?" Ben asked. "I see this place is up for auction at the end of the month."

"Who'd buy it?" the boy asked back. "No, they don't know we're here. You going to tell them?"

"None of our business," Gary replied. "You here alone?"

"That's none of your business either."

"Fair enough." Gary looked around. "You want to get the power back on. Nights'll be turning cold soon."

"Thanks for your concern," the boy replied, sarcastically.

Gary and Ben glanced at each other.

"We'll see ourselves out," Gary told the lad. "What do you reckon?" he asked Ben when they were outside the squat.

"He's up to no good. Did you clock his name?"

"Yeah."

"That was a Mansfield accent," Ben said. He should know. Ben had been born and brought up in one of the few black families living in Mansfield. "I'll bet if we check the PNC we'll find out that he's got a record there. He didn't want us to see the other bloke in the house. Hear that noise?"

"I did. Sounded like his mate was hiding stuff in case we decided to look around without a warrant. They must think we're thick."

Ben nodded.

"Thick as thieves. Small-time villains, I guess that's all they are. Still, we'd better keep an eye out, put a notice on the bulletin board when we get in. You never know…"

Back at the station, Paul Grace listened to Ben and Gary with interest.

"I'm going round that way tonight, so I'll take a

look as I'm passing. Do you think it's worth applying for a search warrant?"

Gary shook his head.

"We checked out this J Hatton. First name Joseph. Aged eighteen. He's got form for breaking and entering, also receiving. Did six months in Glen Parva. If there's anything bent in there, he's experienced enough to have moved it by now."

"Did you see anything when you were at the train driver's place last night?" Ben asked the boss. Grace had mentioned the surveillance at that morning's briefing. The Inspector shook his head.

"No. But I'll give it another go tonight."

"Unpaid overtime," Gary commented afterwards. "He must be mad."

"Maybe that's how he got to be an Inspector so young," Ben commented.

"Your birthday?" Neil said to Dean. "Sure you can have a party. But why here? It's so small. Wouldn't you be better off hiring a place in town? Clare and Ruth had their twenty-firsts at—"

"I don't want lots of people," Dean told him. "I don't have that many friends. I thought, just a few blokes from the team and their girlfriends. You, Melanie and a couple of your friends."

"All right," Neil said. "Saturday night. Let's hope you have a decent result from Leicester to celebrate."

Saturday's visit to nearby Leicester was the closest Forest usually got to a local derby now that Notts County languished in a much lower division. However, Forest were about to play County in a Coca-Cola cup second leg, the first time they'd met in donkey's years. Forest were already one goal up from the away leg, so, Neil feared, it would be a walk-over.

"Which members of the team will you invite?" Neil asked, as Dean got ready for training.

"All of them, I guess, but half won't come. Jeff will. And Stuart. Chris. And Umberto. I already asked him if he was doing anything and he's up for it."

"Umberto Capricio in my house," Neil said, jokily. "Pity I'm not still going out with Clare, the Italian girl I told you about. She'd be impressed."

"Invite her," Dean told him. "Mind you, Umberto has quite a reputation where the ladies are concerned."

"Didn't you tell me he was living with some model in a luxury house by the river?"

Dean grinned. "That was last week. The latest story is that she walked out after finding him in bed with her younger sister."

"Ouch," Neil muttered, then seemed to worry. "He'd better bring someone with him. I don't want him putting the moves on Melanie."

"By the way," Dean said, his voice becoming

anxious, "is there anything else on how Mary died? I've been wondering…"

Neil shook his head. "The boss has taken me off the case. The inquest isn't for a couple of weeks but, without any definite evidence of a burglary, it's bound to go down as accidental death."

Dean nodded soberly.

"There is one thing," Neil said. "I've been meaning to ask you – was Mary in the habit of keeping her back door unlocked?"

"Not normally," Dean said. "But sometimes she did if she was in and you know…"

"Hanging washing out to dry, that kind of thing?"

"Yeah. Was the door unlocked?"

"It was," Neil said. "Someone could have broken the glass, reached in, and turned the key. Or Mary could have opened it herself, earlier. We'll probably never know."

Dean's taxi arrived, stopping him from having to make any further comment. Neil was still suspicious, Dean could tell. But the inquest was weeks away and the police were overstretched as ever. Who cared what happened to a poor pensioner? Easiest to put it down as an accident. Unless Dean found out something different. Yet even if Joe and Darren were responsible, could Dean tell on them? Darren, he would shop any time, but Joe was almost family. And Joe knew all of Dean's secrets.

Put it out of your mind, Dean told himself. *Think*

about something else. You're having a party. In a way, Dean was looking forward to his party. He'd never had one before. Joe and Darren wouldn't be gate-crashing it, that was for sure. They were going to be too busy.

Natalie Loscoe sat in the visitor's gallery with Curt Wilder. Her father had pleaded guilty. His solicitor had told him that he'd probably be sentenced to a year in prison, but would be out in six months, maybe less.

"This sort of crime is on the increase," the judge said. "It was a fraud which wasted an enormous amount of police time, impeded a major crime investigation and nearly succeeded in extorting an enormous amount of money from an insurance company. For a man in your position, with huge sums at his disposal, there are no excuses. Therefore, I sentence you to the maximum amount allowed by the law: five years."

"*Five years?*" Gordon Loscoe looked like he was about to faint. They took him down.

"He wasn't expecting that," Curt said, when they were outside. Mum had stayed to talk to the lawyers.

"He wasn't," Natalie agreed. She thought her dad deserved to go to prison. He was a fat, selfish slob and she hated him most of the time. But she didn't think that he deserved five years.

"What are you and your mum gonna do now?"

Curt asked.

"Dunno," Natalie said. "There's someone interested in the house. We'll move as soon as possible. Mum wants to rent a flat in Mapperley Park. We looked round it yesterday – two floors, three bedrooms."

"Posh."

"Sort of. But there's no schools nearby. Most of the kids there go to private schools. I might have to go to Rushcliffe again."

That was the school she went to before Dad won the Lottery. Curt used to go there too, but he'd been thrown out – Natalie didn't know why. Now he went to a special unit, when he could be bothered, while she hadn't been to her poncy private school since Dad got arrested. He hadn't paid the fees for this term anyway.

"Want to come back to mine?" she asked.

"Nah. Let's go to mine. We can walk it."

"Won't your mum be in?"

"No. She's round Uncle Eddie's. And Julie's gone to her mate's for tea."

"All right then, let's go."

Leaving the court building, Natalie spotted the Inspector who'd given her a lift home once, the one who'd been responsible for catching Dad. Grace. He came over and spoke to them.

"Bit of a shock for you, Natalie. I thought, with the confession, he'd get less."

"I guess he got what was coming to him," Natalie said.

"I wanted to know if either of you have seen Eddie Broom recently. He's a friend of both your families, isn't he?"

Natalie looked at Curt and he gave his head the smallest of shakes.

"I haven't seen him," she said.

"Me neither," Curt told him.

"Isn't he friendly with your mother?"

Curt gave the policeman a dirty look.

"He hasn't been round for weeks."

"All right, thanks. Sorry about your dad, Natalie." He walked away.

"I'll bet he's really sorry," Natalie commented, sarcastically, when the Inspector was out of earshot. "What's the story with Uncle Eddie? Where is he living?"

"Search me," Curt said. "Mum goes to see him two or three times a week, says he's working round here. But she never says where."

"Is she serious about him?"

"Mum? She's serious about anyone who'll have her."

"That's a horrible thing to say about your mother!" Natalie protested.

"You've never had a hiding from her," Curt said.

Natalie knew that Shirley bashed Curt around sometimes and he hated her for it. But Natalie could see both sides. Curt could be a right swine. It must be hard, having a son like him and no man about the place. No money, either. But now the swine put his arm around Natalie's waist and spoke to her tenderly.

"I'm sorry about your dad. Don't worry. I'll look after you."

"Thanks."

When Curt was with Natalie, he could be an angel. Her guardian angel. She didn't know what she'd do without him.

"Nice place you've got here," Dean told Umberto.

The Italian player, a former European footballer of the year, showed Dean around his house, which overlooked the Trent.

"Don't you get people trying to look inside?"

"Yes," Umberto told him. "But the garden is very private."

"It's good of you to show me round," Dean said. He'd felt awkward, angling for the invitation. The Italian had seemed surprised by his interest.

"You're welcome," Umberto said. "Would you like to see my paintings?"

"Er, sure."

Dean followed his teammate into a room with a triple lock. Umberto shrugged as he opened it. "Insurance requirement." The room, a former scullery, was deep and cool. It had subdued lighting.

"This is a Picasso," Umberto told Dean. "So is this. One early, one late. I'm looking to buy something from his middle period, but I need another big signing fee first, eh?" Dean laughed. He'd heard of Picasso, though the paintings meant nothing to him.

"This is a Matisse. This is by a young British painter, Duncan Higgins. And this is my favourite, a Magritte."

"You've spent ten years playing and you've put all your money into … paintings?"

Umberto smiled at Dean's question. "Can you tell me of a better investment?"

There were some other pictures which Umberto didn't bother showing off. They didn't look like art to Dean. He followed the footballer out and watched as Umberto locked the door carefully.

This guy was out of Joe and Darren's league, Dean decided. He couldn't understand what he was doing here, setting the footballer up to be burgled. What he really wanted was to tell Joe and Darren that it was useless, that they'd never get into the house and there was nothing worth stealing anyway. After all, what would they do with fancy paintings?

Above them, a door slammed.

"Girlfriend?" Dean asked.

Umberto smiled. He had a very charming smile. Everyone liked him, despite the fact that he earned as much as the rest of the squad put together.

"My mother," Umberto told him. "My father died

last year and, since then, my mother moves between me and my two sisters. She likes England and I have the most room, so she stays with me longest."

"No live-in girlfriend, then?"

Dean expected a man like Umberto to have a constant stream of beautiful girls on tap.

"You heard the story about the two beautiful sisters, huh?"

"I heard it."

"You shouldn't believe every bit of dressing-room gossip," Umberto said, with a twinkle in his eye.

"Having your mother living with you must cramp your style," Dean commented.

"Not really. She's asleep by ten every night and nothing wakes her. Do you mind? I think I should check on her."

"No problem."

As soon as Umberto left the room, Dean began to look around more carefully. He opened drawers and cupboard doors. Nothing that special. Umberto had a lot of books in Italian. Dean pulled one out. Sometimes, people kept safes and stuff hidden behind bookshelves. Nothing. He checked the next row. Nothing. But, wait, what was that?

Dean could hear the footballer coming back. He stuffed the magazine back where he'd found it. Put together, the magazine and the photographs in the scullery revealed Umberto's secret. Dean hurried quickly to the other end of the room.

"Is she all right?"

"Yes, fine." Umberto joined him by the kitchen door. *Not so close*, Dean wanted to say.

"Is something wrong? You're shivering. Should I turn the air conditioning down?"

"I'm all right," Dean said, moving away and pointing at the wall. "Is that the alarm system? How does it work?"

"I forget," Umberto said. "I never turn it on. The noise it makes scares my mother."

"I'd better be going," Dean said. He followed the Italian out. He could help Joe to burgle him, Dean supposed. But then he remembered Mary, his former landlady, and what had happened to her. What if he helped Joe and Darren break in, and something similar happened to Umberto's mother? He couldn't be responsible for that.

But if he didn't help them, Joe would go to the press or the police or both. His career could be over. As Dean remembered his conversation with Joe and Darren, another thought occurred to him: how did Darren know that Mary had had an accident?

8

Paul considered following Curt and Natalie home, but doubted that he'd learn anything. They'd been lying about not having seen Eddie Broom, that much had been obvious. However, even if the kids knew where he lived, Paul doubted that he could get either of them to tell him the address. Paul was coming to a conclusion about the question of Shirley Wilder and Eddie Broom. If he was right, the answer had been staring him in the face. Watching the house was a waste of time. What he needed to do was follow Shirley.

Time was running out. He needed to get on it tonight. But Paul couldn't keep tabs on Shirley by himself. For a start, he was on duty until ten. He decided to ring Clare at home. Her working day was over. Maybe she'd be willing to help tonight.

Before Paul could dial the number, there was a call for him. It was Nigel.

"Thought you might like to save yourself some time. It's Shirley you're after, right?"

"Right."

"Then there's no point in watching the house tonight, 'cos she's going away for a few days."

"How do you know?" Paul asked. "Who with?"

"She didn't tell me that. But a fella, from the way she was talking when she bumped into me earlier."

"Question is," Paul said, "where's she going?"

"I can help you with that, too."

"How do you mean?"

"Shirley's taking the seven-fifteen to Glasgow tonight."

"How...?"

"I know because she asked if I'd be driving the train."

"Yes!" Paul slapped his hands together. If the motorway team were planning a robbery and Eddie was their reconnaissance man, Eddie would be setting himself up with another watertight alibi. What better way than to take his girlfriend somewhere several hours away?

Paul called CID, but it was too late – only the night crime officer was on duty. He could call the task force who were supposed to be investigating the team, but they would never get over from

Birmingham in time, even presuming that they could be bothered to. So he called Clare.

"You went to Umberto Capricio's house?" Neil asked, incredulously.

"Yeah," Dean told him, without enthusiasm. "I asked him what the place was like and he invited me round."

"And what is it like?"

"He has these paintings…"

"A footballer collecting modern art," Neil said when he'd finished. "That's weird. I mean, I remember reading that one the players was in a punk group, but collecting art – he must be rolling in it."

"I guess," Dean said, quietly. He had to ring Joe. It didn't look like Neil was going out tonight, so he'd better use a phone box.

"I need to go to the shop," he told his landlord. "Get you anything?"

"No, thanks. Are you all right? You look a bit pale."

"Just training hard. Leicester Saturday, Cup replay on Tuesday. It's a big week."

Dean walked to the nearest phone box, which was on the Hucknall Road. Joe was on a mobile number (nicked, doubtless) and Dean had to pump in a quid for their short conversation.

"The usual. Hi-fi. Lots of video stuff. No computer, but I reckon there's some jewellery upstairs."

"Safe?"

"Probably. But I couldn't ask him where it was and what the combination is, now could I?"

"Anything else?"

"There's a room full of paintings, but it's locked."

"Not interested."

"They're worth millions. If you could get a couple out without damaging them, you could hold them to ransom."

"What do you think we are — master criminals? Where's he keep his drugs?"

"No idea. He didn't offer me anything, so maybe he doesn't use."

"What about the alarm?"

"He never has it on. The front of the house looks pretty secure, but there's a downstairs toilet, with a window partly shaded by a tree. You could take it out, no problem. I knackered the window lock for you just before I left. I doubt he'll notice. He's got three or four toilets. It didn't look like he used that one much."

"Nice one. We owe you."

"You know exactly what you owe me. After this, you stay away from me. No talking to the press about my past, or I tell them that you did this job. In future, if you want to watch me play, do it on TV. OK?"

"OK," Joe said, "if that's the way you want it."

"There's one other thing. His mother lives with him."

"*What?*"

"She's in her sixties. And she goes to bed at half-nine every night. An earthquake wouldn't wake her after ten, according to Umberto. But to be on the safe side, I'd wait until a bit later. Her bedroom's on the left side of the house, above the kitchen. Don't go in there."

Joe mumbled something noncommittal. He would go in the room if he thought that there was something worth taking, Dean realized. His conscience kicked his mouth into action.

"There's something I want to know," he said.

"What?"

"How come Darren knew that my landlady had had an accident?"

There was a pause. Dean wished that he could see Joe's face.

"You'd have to ask him," Joe said. "He told me he'd heard it somewhere."

"Because the police said it was possible there'd been a break-in. If I find out that you two had anything to—"

"Come on," Joe interrupted. "We're old mates. Would I break into your house, huh? You're insulting me."

"Sorry," Dean said, feeling guilty again about having blanked Joe from his life. "That's all, then. If there're any changes, I'll call you on this number."

Dean hung up without giving Joe time to reply.

Despite the blackmail, or whatever you wanted to call it, he felt bad about Joe.

They'd been friends since they were both two years old. From the minute they'd learned to talk, they started goading each other into more and more dangerous games. By the time they were in their teens, the games had started to become real. Dean proved to have a talent for football, but Joe's only talent was for burglary. Joe would kick a ball around with Dean, help him practise. Dean, in return, helped Joe break into houses. Usually, he stood watch, but, a few times, he'd been inside. Luckily, the time Joe got caught, Dean got away and Joe kept his name out of it. Dean owed him for that.

After such a close call, he'd stopped stealing, scared of spending a spell in Glen Parva like Joe and Darren. Dean missed the amphetamine buzz of burglary, but Joe was out of the picture and his football was becoming all-consuming. Mansfield Town showed an interest in him just as Joe got out.

Joe was jealous as hell. His old mate goaded Dean to keep going, to nick cars, do houses. At the very least, he could still keep look-out. Dean did a couple, out of loyalty. Joe had protected him, after all. When it became clear that Dean wasn't interested in burglary, Joe started bringing his new mate Darren along. Dean hated Darren, but he was also relieved. Joe had a new friend and Dean was under less pressure to hang out with him.

For all his faults, Joe was a good laugh. Dean hadn't yet found a new best mate to replace his friendship.

Then there was Umberto Capricio. It was wrong, Dean knew, to betray a teammate. But Umberto could afford to be burgled. Given what he was, the Italian almost deserved to have his house messed up. So, on Saturday night, all debts would be repaid.

Clare parked in the short-stay car park at the front of the station and remained in the car, as Paul had requested. It was five to seven. The train left at quarter past. If Eddie and Shirley weren't here by five past, Clare decided, they weren't coming.

At six minutes past seven, a maroon BMW parked in the spot next to Clare. Eddie Broom got out, alone. What was going on? Clare gave him a moment, then followed him into the station's vast, Victorian booking hall. To deter vagrants and abusers, the space had nowhere to sit down and, at this time, it was deserted. Clare saw Shirley Wilder, standing at one of the ticket windows. Eddie must have dropped her off by the entrance, then parked. There was no way to tell if Shirley was buying one ticket or two. She left, carrying a shoulder bag. Eddie hurried to join her, holding a much heavier suitcase. Clare followed the couple down to platform three, where the Glasgow train was waiting. Both got on it.

Paul joined Clare.

"He's in the short stay?"

"Yes."

"Give me the key to Ruth's car. I want to follow him."

"It looks like he's going with her."

"No. Eddie's keen on his car. He wouldn't leave it there to be towed away."

"It might be stolen."

"No. It's legit, apart from being registered at a false address. Give me the keys."

"You don't know the car," Clare protested. "I'll drive."

A porter began closing the doors on the train. Eddie got out.

"Quick," Paul said. "Kiss me, like you've just met me off a train."

Clare did as he asked. His kiss was passionate, promising. When they pulled apart, Eddie Broom was walking past them, empty-handed. Hand in hand, Clare and Paul followed him. Two minutes later, Ruth's 2CV was following his BMW out of the station car park, with Clare in the driver's seat.

"I hope he isn't going anywhere fast," she told Paul. "Top speed on this car's sixty, and the acceleration's virtually non-existent."

At first, Eddie seemed to be heading towards the Maynard Estate. They followed him down Queen's Road and turned right on to London Road. Then, instead of turning right again, to go into the Meadows, he drove over Trent Bridge, past the Forest ground, turning down Radcliffe Road.

"He's heading back towards Bingham, where I spotted him before," Paul guessed. But he wasn't. Just before the road became a dual carriageway, Eddie signalled right, turning into the drive of one of the big, semi-detached houses. Clare kept on the A52 until the roundabout, then turned around.

"Let me out on the corner," Paul said. "I'll try and get a closer look."

"You've got your radio?"

"Yes. Why don't you get over to West Bridgford CID, find out what they know about the house and who lives there?"

"I'd better contact the task force in Solihull, too."

"Leave it till morning. Maybe I'll be able to get you some overtime authorized."

"I'm not doing this for the money," she said, and kissed him on the lips. "Be careful. Don't get arrested again." Paul laughed and began to walk back up Radcliffe Road. Clare drove past the house which Eddie had gone into. His car was already in the garage.

At West Bridgford Police Station she checked the occupancy of the house on the electoral register. There were five different names, none of which was Eddie Broom's. She guessed that it was divided into bedsits.

"Out of uniform, duck?" a sergeant asked her.

"I'm in CID now. Does this address ring a bell?"

"Can't say it does. But we have an index. Give me five minutes."

Clare did a PNC check of the names on the electoral register while she waited. Nothing.

The sergeant returned. "Not much for you. Back in July, someone reported a break-in at that address, but when an officer went round, the occupant said that nothing had been stolen, it was only kids larking about."

"Do you know the name of this occupant who was interviewed?"

"According to this, the guy's name was Stevens, Christopher Stevens."

The name meant nothing to Clare.

9

Once he'd got out of the car, Paul didn't know what he was doing. He was off his patch, out of uniform and on duty. Getting arrested was the sort of accident which could happen to an Inspector once. If it happened a second time, he would look a complete fool.

There was a thick hedge in front of the house. Paul tried to peer through it, looking to see how many doorbells there were. Four or five. The house had a double garage which appeared new, or at least its door did. All of the windows were hidden by filthy net curtains. The windows themselves looked like they hadn't been cleaned this year. The house looked unoccupied. But Eddie Broom had gone in there.

Paul had visited houses on Radcliffe Road. Most had long gardens at the back. He could either interview the neighbours, or find whoever lived in the house behind this one, on Davies Road, and see if the house could be watched from there. No one put lace curtains on their back windows.

He considered checking the house next door now, but it seemed more prudent to wait and see what Clare had found out. He walked past the house and turned up Priory Road, then got out his radio.

"Find anything?" his girlfriend asked.

"No. You?"

"If the house is still flats, they aren't rented out any more. A man calling himself Christopher Stevens was living there in July, when there was a reported break-in. That's all."

Paul joined Clare at the station, where he briefed the West Bridgford night shift to keep an eye on the house where Broom seemed to be hiding. Then he and Clare looked up Christopher Stevens on the police national computer. Unfortunately, it was a common name and there was no one on the computer at that address. Nor was there anyone of that name who had a record which suggested that they belonged to the motorway team. All of which proved nothing, they agreed, as Paul drove Clare home.

"Come back to my place?" he suggested.

"All right," she said, "you persuaded me. But stop in Forest Fields so I can get some stuff."

At Clare's house, Ruth was on her way up to bed.

"How's Ben?" she asked. "I hope you're looking after him."

"He's fine," Paul assured her. "Doesn't he call you every night when he gets off?"

Ruth smiled. "We're not like you two, in the first flush of romance, you know. We don't live in each other's pockets."

"Sorry I spoke," Paul said.

Was he seeing too much of Clare? He hadn't been anywhere without her since they started going out. *So what?* Paul thought, as Clare came bounding down the stairs, an overnight bag in her hands and a big smile on her face. You couldn't see too much of someone when you were head over heels in love. He wanted her with him more of the time, not less.

"Let's go," he said.

Ruth woke at five, half an hour before she needed to. Paul Grace's words needled her as she took a shower: *Doesn't he call you every night when he gets off?* Until recently, Ben used to do just that. Since they got back from holiday, she'd hardly seen him. True, there'd been that night round at Paul Grace's and a drink after work before that. But they hadn't had sex once since the holiday. Not that she was counting.

Snap out of it! Ruth told herself. Maybe you could see too much of a person. After all that time in each other's company, a bit of a gap was called for. That was probably all it was. And the last thing she wanted to do was blow everything by being jealous.

Ruth went to work. She was fed up with her shift. Since Roy Tate retired, there was no one she really got on with, and to make things worse, there were blokes she couldn't stand. When they discussed it on holiday, Ben suggested that she ought to apply for a transfer if things didn't get better. Things, if anything, were getting worse.

"Your suntan's starting to fade," Mike Bingley, her partner, commented when she got into the parade room.

"How about your boyfriend?" Stuart Webster asked. "Is his fading, too?"

Ruth turned round and told him where to go. Stuart shrugged it off.

"Touchy this morning," Mike commented.

"He could get a reprimand for that kind of remark," Ruth told him.

"Only if someone reported him," Mike said, "and there are no black officers in this shift. Unless you were thinking of making trouble..."

"You can go screw yourself, too," Ruth told him, and went to the loo. Inside the cubicle, she burst into tears. It wasn't easy, going out with a black bloke when you were in the force – even if he was in the police himself. It might be easier if she could talk it over with Ben more, but Ben didn't like to

95

talk about issues of colour. He said she should ignore everything to do with race. That was what he did. But it wasn't so easy.

Ruth wanted to see Ben, but his working day started as hers finished. After today, though, she had a couple of rest days. She would see him then. And if there was a problem between them, they would work it out. That was what grown ups did, Ruth told herself. She dried her eyes and went back to the parade room.

"Sorry I snapped at you," Ruth told Mike. It was always best to keep on the right side of your partner, never mind how much of a deadbeat he was.

"I understand," Mike said. "Time of the month, eh?"

Ruth gritted her teeth and began work. She would put in for that transfer today.

As soon as Clare got to the CID office in the morning, she rang Phil Church, her liaison at the Solihull task force. He seemed underwhelmed by the news that they had found Eddie Broom's hideaway.

"We've also managed to place someone who used the name Stevens. I think that they're planning another job and this is their base. Maybe it's always been their base."

"All right. I'll pass the information on. But do nothing until you hear from us."

Frustrated, Clare put the phone down. They must get leads all the time, she told herself, but this one seemed so good, so strong. She wouldn't let it go. While she was staring into space, DI Greasby stopped at her desk.

"Penny for them?"

"Sorry. I was miles away."

"A little bird tells me that you were putting in some unpaid overtime last night."

"You have eyes everywhere, sir?"

"Everywhere you can think of, and then some. Your old boss phoned me five minutes ago, asked me to give you the day to do some work in West Bridgford. We don't cover West Bridgford, I told him."

"It's a long story."

"I've heard it. You can have today, and today only. But take Neil with you. Those boys – on the off chance that you've got the right boys – are probably armed. Got me?"

"A hundred per cent. I'm on my way."

"So where are we going?" Neil asked, five minutes later.

"Davies Road. That's where the neighbour who reported the break-in lives. I want to ask her if she's seen anything else, and whether we can spy out of the back window."

"And what are we hoping to see?"

"I'm hoping to get a glimpse of what they're doing in there. You're going to watch the front, see who goes in and out."

"How come you get the indoor assignment?" Neil complained.

"Eddie's seen me before, in the casino. There's a chance he'll work out what's going on if he notices me watching his house."

"Whereas I…?"

"Will use your ingenuity to park the car and keep your head down."

"Praying that they don't notice."

"Park further down the street. Why should they notice?"

The woman who lived behind the suspect house was happy to let Clare use a back bedroom to spy on it.

"I'm sure they had a break-in during July," she said. "A few minutes after I heard the glass breaking, I heard someone running. And the couple who live next door but one say they found some blood on their fence. But would the police come and look at it? Would they hell!"

"No crime was reported. Have you noticed anything else … unusual about that house?"

"Only that it seems to be empty most of the time. It used to be flats. You'd think with the housing shortage that the owners would rent some of it out, wouldn't you?"

Clare brought with her a CID video camera with an eighty times digital zoom. She could look right into the back rooms of the suspect house. She could get a close up on a face. But the neighbour was right. The place looked empty. One window had the curtains drawn. The other rooms looked unoccupied, except for the kitchen, where a kettle was steaming. Beside it stood a packet of tea bags, an open carton of milk and two mugs. Clare focused right in on the mugs. They were giveaways from a building firm.

Eddie Broom came into the kitchen, made two mugs of tea, then took them to the front of the house, out of Clare's view. She radioed Neil.

"Anything?"

"Nothing at all."

She told him what she'd seen.

"You've no idea who the second man is?"

"None at all."

"This must be it, their base."

Clare agreed. "Could be a long day."

"So, are you coming to my party on Saturday?"

Clare thought she'd turned this down already. "I don't think it's Paul's idea of fun."

"Bring someone else, then. Ruth and Ben are coming."

"I'll see."

Neil wanted to show off his famous footballers but was spoiling the effect by trying too hard, as usual. Still, Clare might go, if he wanted her to so much.

"The garage door's opening," Neil radioed her, ten minutes later. "Eddie's coming out. I might be able to get a look at what's in the garage. No. Someone's closing the door behind him, or maybe it's automatic. Think I should follow him?"

"I dunno," Clare said.

They risked missing a look at the other guy. Clare could only see what happened at the back of the house. Neil made the decision.

"He might be about to visit the place they plan to do. I'm off."

"Are you sure?"

There was no reply. Clare sat in the room alone, watching the kitchen window, wishing that she had some action. Nothing happened.

Over the next two hours, Neil radioed Clare regularly to let her know where he was. Eddie had been to a car wash, then stopped for a drink at the Test match pub. He'd driven out to the country, passing the spot where the gang had met up before, but didn't go there. Then he stopped for a while by a big house in Gamston, maybe with a view to burglary. Then he was off into the city, parking in a multi-storey. Neil parked on the same level, and waited. Eddie Broom returned three quarters of an hour later, had a conversation on his mobile phone, then drove back to West Bridgford. He pointed a device at the garage doors and they opened automatically. Neil saw another car in the garage which meant that more of the gang had arrived. Neil didn't get time to make out the licence plate.

"Seen anything?" he asked Clare over the radio.

"No one," she said, bored out of her skull in between calls. "Nothing. But, hold on … there's someone coming. It's only Eddie. He's putting the kettle on."

"How many mugs?" Neil asked, urgently.

"Be patient," Clare told him. "He's washing them out now. One. Two. Three."

"Three?"

"No. Wait. He's opening a cupboard, getting another one. That's it. Four."

"We've got them!" Neil said, excitedly. "The whole team! What a result!"

10

"Got a little job for you," Grace told Ben and Gary. "A building society's auctioning this property tomorrow. They have reason to believe that there are squatters occupying it. They want to clean the house out before the viewing tomorrow, so they'll go along with a cleaning crew and a couple of heavies. You'll be there to keep the peace, so to speak."

"Waste of time, if you ask me," Gary said.

Ben was surprised to hear him giving the boss backchat, but Grace didn't respond.

"You know what'll happen," Ben told Gary, as they drove over to the Maynard Estate. "Those two tosspots from earlier will be out somewhere, so their stuff'll be thrown on to the street, and we'll pick up the bother when they get back and discover that it's all been nicked."

"Probably nicked it themselves in the first place," Gary commented.

But the house wasn't empty. When the building society men broke the door down, the people in the street heard loud swearing from above.

"You can't do that! This is our home!" The tirade finished.

"Not any more, it isn't."

The two boys left sheepishly enough in the end, carting their stuff into an ancient Ford Escort. Ben did a radio check. The car was registered to a Darren Braithwaite of Mansfield. He asked the younger of the two lads for his name and address.

"Name's Darren Braithwaite. That's my address, over there." Bits of old furniture were being thrown into a skip across the road.

"Do you have a Mansfield address?"

"Only my parents."

He gave the address. It was the same as the one the DVLC had given.

"All right," Ben said, "off you go. But for your next squat, choose somewhere off my beat. OK?"

"Think I'll take a quick look around before the cleaners go in," Gary told Ben when the boys had gone.

"Be my guest."

Ben went to disperse the small crowd which had

gathered to watch the show.

"There's nothing more to see," he assured them. "Move along."

One person remained when the rest had gone.

"Hello, Julie," Ben said. "No Tammy today?"

"Curt and Natalie are looking after her."

"Shouldn't they be at school?"

Julie laughed.

"How's your mum?" Ben asked her.

"She's gone on holiday."

"Where'd she go?" Ben asked.

"Glasgow."

"On her own?"

"With a friend. So it's just me and Tammy in the house most of the time." Was that an invitation? Ben had a brief glimpse into her wide, doe eyes.

"Take a look at this," Gary called, as Julie turned and walked away. He was holding a football, signed by the entire Nottingham Forest cup-winning team of a few seasons back. Alongside the players' name was a dedication: *To Mary*.

"I wonder who Mary is," Ben said.

"And what those young thugs were doing with her ball," Gary added.

"Have you rung Birmingham again?" Paul Grace asked Clare, over the phone.

"Phil Church was on his lunch when I called. He's meant to be ringing me back. I said it was urgent."

"How many of the gang did you get on video?"
Paul asked.

"Only Eddie. You're still the only person who's
seen them all."

"That's bothers me. It's almost as though they
know they're being watched."

"How would they know that?" Clare asked, reas-
suringly.

"I suppose you're right. Is Neil still watching the
front?"

"Yes. Do you want me to go back and start film-
ing again?"

"No. Let Birmingham take over the surveillance.
They'll get the glory, so they might as well do the
rest of the boring stuff."

"What about when Neil goes off duty?"

"They should be able to get someone over there
by then. Tell them to call me if they need as-
sistance." He drew breath, then added, "Looks like
another long day."

"Why don't I let myself into your place," Clare
suggested, "cook you a late supper?"

"That'd be great."

Clare liked sharing a house, but she also liked
having Paul to herself sometimes. She put the phone
down and, immediately, it rang again. Phil Church.

"They're all in there," Clare informed him. "That
means they must be planning a job tonight or
tomorrow."

"Or they could simply be having a meeting."

"Even if that's all it is, you'll be able to catch them, identify them. We've got someone watching the house until five. Can you cover it after that?"

"If we think it's worthwhile."

"Look, you can either get a warrant and search the place, or follow the gang when they do the job, but you've got to do one or the other."

Clare heard the DC taking a deep breath fifty miles away.

"Listen, *Detective*." He said the word with a spin which suggested he knew that Clare wasn't a real detective. "Your Eddie Broom and his colleagues might – and I stress the word *might* – be the motor-way team. Leave it with us. I'll take it to my boss. If he thinks it's worth following, we'll be over."

"Keep me informed, will you, as a courtesy?"

"Certainly. I've got your home number."

"I'll be at a different one after nine."

Church took it. "Boyfriend?"

"Actually, yes."

"Not a certain Inspector Paul Grace, by any chance?"

"How do you…?" Clare began to ask, embar-rassed.

"No secrets in the police force. You're obviously an ambitious girl."

Church hung up before Clare could think of a sufficiently barbed reply.

*   *   *

Dean had just got in from training when the door-bell went. No one had visited him at his new home yet, so it was probably for Neil, who was due home. Melanie, maybe. Dean was hoping that she would bring a friend or two to his party on Saturday.

It wasn't Melanie. It was Joe.

"How did you know I was here?" Dean asked angrily.

"I phoned your mum." Dean had told her not to tell anybody, but Joe could talk the birds out of the trees when the mood took him. "Aren't you going to invite me in?"

Dean looked around.

"Darren's parking the car."

Joe stepped into the living-room.

"Nice place. Got a spare bedroom? Darren and I don't mind sharing."

"No," Dean said. "My landlord'll be back in a minute. You don't want to mess with him. He's a…"

"Another OAP?" Joe interrupted. "Look, Dean. You and me are a team. I'll dump Darren if you like. We can go into business after this job. Legit."

"I've got a career," Dean told him. "Anyway, you promised, I get you into Umberto's and you leave me alone."

"Circumstances have changed," Joe told him. "I'm homeless, for a start."

"Your mum'd take you back. We had a deal, Joe."

"We're old friends, Dean. I don't want to mess that up."

"How did you find this place?" Dean asked, changing the subject. They were interrupted before Joe could answer.

"Hello there."

Both youths looked round. Neil Foster stood in the doorway.

"Bit cold, with this open."

"There's someone else coming," Joe told him, all charm. "He's parking the car. I'm Joe, an old friend of Dean's."

"Pleased to meet you. I'm Neil Foster."

Dean squirmed as Joe shook Neil's hand. Darren walked in and looked taken aback.

"And this is Darren."

"Sorry about the parking round here," Neil said. "Sometimes I have to go two streets away myself."

The four of them stood awkwardly. It was up to Dean to say something. He wanted to signal to the two lads that Neil was a policeman, but the looks on their faces indicated that they'd already worked that out.

"We'd better be going," Joe said. "Give us a call tomorrow, Dean, all right?"

"I'll do that."

He was meant to phone when Umberto arrived so that they'd know when the coast was clear.

"See you at the party tomorrow night," Neil said, as the two youths scurried out of the house.

"Oh, right," Joe said, with a sickly smile. "Tomorrow night."

"Good friends?" Neil asked when they'd gone.

"Not really," Dean said. "I knew them in Mansfield. They just dropped by to say hello, see if I could get them some tickets for the cup match."

"Hope I didn't drop you in it by mentioning the party," Neil said.

"No," Dean assured him, "you didn't. They'd already made other plans."

11

Ben didn't know why he was knocking on Julie Wilder's door. He certainly wouldn't be doing it if his partner were with him. But Gary was at the city ground. There was a supporters' club meeting, and he wanted to see if anyone could identify the Mary who'd had a football signed for her. The chances of finding the ball's owner were slim. Fans all over the city had signed balls and this one hadn't been reported stolen. But those two lads were wrong 'uns. It would be nice to nick them and return the ball.

Julie looked surprised to see him. She was dressed unappealingly, in old jeans and a scruffy sweatshirt. She went to the kitchen to put the kettle on, and when she came back, she had brushed her hair.

"How was your holiday?" she asked.

"All right."

Beach holidays weren't for him. By the end of this one, Ben had been bored: bored with the beach, bored with the books he'd taken to read ... bored with Ruth, too, if he was honest with himself. But he didn't say any of this.

"I didn't get to go on mine," Julie told him.

"I heard."

Ben didn't know all the details, but he knew that Julie had never got the £50,000 she won on the National Lottery. While Ben was in Ibiza, he'd imagined Julie in Spain, being chased by suntanned youths. But she'd remained trapped on the Maynard Estate. He looked at her longingly. There were no expectations in her eyes.

"So why did you come round?" she asked.

"Because you suggested it. I thought maybe you had some information."

Julie looked disappointed, but not much.

"I'm not a police informer," she said.

"I didn't mean..." Ben floundered for words.

"But I'll help you if I can."

Ben remembered Inspector Grace's surveillance.

"I wondered whether you'd seen Eddie Broom recently."

"No, I haven't."

Ben nodded. That was that, then. He would drink his tea as quickly as possible and get out. He shouldn't have come.

"But my mum has," Julie added.

"Really?"

"He's got a place in West Bridgford somewhere."

This was news to Ben.

"He won't come here, because he thinks the house might be watched. He's even had to change his car, Mum says. So she goes there, spends the night sometimes."

"You don't know the address?"

"No. But he's not there now, anyway. Mum told me today."

"Then where is he?"

"At the station. He's catching the sleeper to Glasgow, joining Mum tomorrow."

Ben worked out what this meant. He'd heard that Shirley had gone to Glasgow. If Eddie was joining her tonight, it meant that the motorway team's next raid was either tonight or tomorrow night, while Eddie had an airtight alibi.

"Why didn't they travel together?" Ben asked.

"You'd have to ask Uncle Eddie that. Not that he'd tell you. He's very cagey about his plans, even with Mum." Julie frowned. "You're pretty cagey too, aren't you?"

"People have said that."

"What's Uncle Eddie been up to?"

Ben shrugged. "Nothing, probably."

"You're not telling the truth."

Ben gave a rueful smile. He didn't like lying to

her, but it was his job. "Maybe I'm not. But you really don't want to know." He looked at his watch. "I'd better go."

She showed him to the door. "Come again, if you like."

"Thanks."

Ben walked briskly away, trying to shake off the thought of Julie, standing so close that he could smell her. Nothing was going to happen between them, he reminded himself. Even if, eventually, he split up with Ruth, Julie was entirely wrong for him. It didn't matter how much he fancied her. She was on his beat. She was too young and too poor, with no education and a nine-months-old baby. Also, her whole family were mixed up with crime, even if she wasn't herself.

He radioed Paul Grace. "I've got some information for you."

Gary drew a complete blank with the football.

"Mary's not a popular name for young girls these days," the secretary told him. "Come back Monday morning when the office is open and I'll give you a print-out of all the Marys who were in the Supporter's club that year."

"I'd appreciate that," Gary said, then remembered he wasn't on duty Monday. "Actually, I'd better make it Wednesday."

"Or we could just take the ball off your hands,

put a notice in the next newsletter."

"That might be the most sensible thing." Gary considered. "Trouble is, the ball's evidence. It was almost certainly stolen. I'd better hang on to it. Why don't I come back on Wednesday, like you suggested?"

There was a commotion behind him. Gary turned to see half of the women in the room – from the very young to the middle aged – rushing towards the door.

"What's that?"

"A couple of the players always come along to these meetings, sign autographs. Looks like Umberto's made it. He only lives down the road."

Now Gary spotted the tall, handsome player. With his long, curly hair and the wicked twinkle in his eyes, Umberto Capricio looked more like a pop star than a football player.

"If there's nothing else…"

"No. That's fine," Gary said. "Call me at the station if anything occurs to you." He took a wistful look at the Italian footballer, then went back to his beat.

Clare had wild mushroom risotto waiting for Paul when he got home. As they ate, he told her about his day, concluding with Ben's information about Eddie Broom.

"It's the confirmation we needed. The gang are using that house and it looks like they're doing a job tonight or tomorrow night."

"So Eddie's on the night train now?" Clare said. "What did Birmingham think of that?"

"I got Charlton on a mobile. He said they'd watch the house and apply for a search warrant. He'll call if anything's going off. So we'd better not drink any more of this wine. We might need our wits about us for a dawn raid."

Clare corked the bottle and they collapsed on to the sofa. Paul flicked through all the TV channels. There was nothing on they wanted to watch, so Clare looked through the discs in his CD tower. She picked one by REM.

"I didn't think that this was your kind of thing."

"It belongs to an ex. She forgot to take it with her."

Tired as she was, Clare didn't miss the implication behind what he'd just said.

"She used to live here?"

"Not here. In the place I had before."

Noisily, the CD began. Clare turned it down.

"I didn't know that you'd ever lived with someone," she said, choosing her words carefully and not looking him in the eyes.

"You never asked," Paul protested. "It wasn't for long. We got on each other's nerves."

"Was she in the job?"

Paul shook his head.

"She was ... is a nurse. Both working shifts, we

hardly ever saw each other. I think that's why it lasted as long as it did."

"You were in love with her?"

"I thought I was."

Clare felt threatened. If he could fall out of love so easily, what hopes should she have? Paul came over to where she was sitting on the carpet and put an arm around her.

"Darling, being with her was nothing like this."

Clare smiled. He had never called her *darling* before. She liked it.

"Who left who?" she asked.

"She announced one day that she was interested in dating a doctor where she worked, and she moved back into nurses' quarters that day. I think she's married now. After that I... Do you really want to know all this?"

"Yes. Yes, I do."

So it all came out. Paul told her the history of his love-life. There had been two women after the nurse and a long gap before he started going out with Clare. Then he told her about the women before the nurse. He went all the way back to his first kiss, aged fifteen. When he was done, Clare told him about her boyfriends. It didn't take nearly as long, but then she was a few years younger than him. By the time they'd finished, it was two in the morning.

"Stay here," Paul asked, in bed. "Don't go home, ever."

"Do you know what you're asking?" Clare said.

She was very tired and didn't know if he meant marriage or living together. She didn't know what he thought the difference was.

"I know what I'm asking. Do you?"

"I think so," Clare said. He wanted her with him all the time. That was the only important thing, wasn't it? "Ask me again when I'm awake."

"All right," he said, gently. The last thing she remembered before going to sleep was him kissing the nape of her neck.

They were woken at five by the phone. Clare answered it. DCI Charlton.

"Rendezvous at West Bridgford station in half an hour. We've got the warrant and we're going in."

"Did they do a job last night?" Clare asked.

"No. Nothing."

She and Paul arrived at the station five minutes early.

"Did anyone leave the house last night?" Paul asked Charlton.

"Not while we were watching."

"Which was when, exactly?"

"From ten onwards."

Paul stared at him in disbelief.

"But that means the house was unattended for five hours!"

The Chief Inspector didn't seem bothered.

"The team do all their jobs just before midnight. Ten was early enough to catch them before they left. Getting there any earlier would only have drawn more attention to ourselves."

"And did you see anything?" Paul asked.

"A couple of lights on at the front. They went out just after twelve. But I had someone there all night, to be on the safe side. Also, I've already placed a couple of people in the back garden opposite, just in case any of them try to scarper that way. Everybody ready?"

As they drove along Radcliffe Road, a pale sun was preparing to rise over Lady Bay. Milk floats were beginning their rounds. The night shift were back at the station, looking forward to their beds, but the morning shift hadn't set out yet. This was the time when a criminal would least expect a knock on the door.

When they arrived at the house there was already a large police presence. A van full of uniforms blocked the driveway. Charlton, Church and two others were in one car, Paul and Clare in another. As they got out, a third vehicle pulled up.

"I don't believe this!" Clare said to Paul. "See who it is?"

Helen Chase, a TV reporter for Central News, was getting out of the news van.

"Give us a moment to set up," she begged DCI Charlton.

"Did you tell them about this?" Paul Grace asked the Chief Inspector.

"Of course. If we bag the motorway team, we want as much publicity as possible."

"But what if—?"

"Listen, Inspector ... Grace, isn't it? You identified this place. You're not telling me that you might have got it wrong, are you?"

"No, but—"

"Right. Everybody ready?"

DCI Charlton walked up to the house and pressed all the doorbells at once. Clare couldn't hear if they rang. When nothing happened, he spoke through a megaphone.

"This is the police. We have a warrant to search this house. If you don't open this door within thirty seconds, it will be broken open."

There was no sound. The only lights which came on were in neighbouring houses. A couple of windows opened. Without waiting the full thirty seconds, DCI Charlton gave the signal. The front door was rammed open. Clare and Paul followed the crowd inside.

Five minutes later, they came back out again, watched by the waiting camera.

"Did you find anything, Inspector?" Helen Chase asked Paul.

"Nothing. The place is completely empty. No story for you, I'm afraid."

"Oh, I don't know about that," the reporter said, turning to the senior officer. "Chief Inspector Charlton, do you still think the motorway team have been using this house as a base?"

"No comment."

Charlton waited until they were back at the station before tearing into Paul and Clare.

"All we found in there was a couple of lights on timers, set to go on at eight and off at twelve. You were set up. I had all these men here on a wild-goose chase! Do me a favour, Inspector. Next time you feel like playing the detective, splash your face with cold water and apply for a transfer to Traffic."

"But if we were set up," Paul pointed out, "it must have been the motorway team. Who else would bother?"

"You tell me," Charlton said. "Made many enemies in the force, have you?"

"No."

"Well, you've made a few today."

Humiliated, Paul took Clare home.

"I'm sure the team were using that house," Clare told him. "Look at the way the garage had been done up. It was fortified, practically a vault."

"Oh, they were using it all right," Paul told her. "But someone told the team that we were on to them."

"Are you sure?"

"I should have worked it out before. Yesterday,

Eddie Broom took Neil on a trip around town. He wanted him out of the way while the others arrived. Then there was the way that Eddie and only Eddie – the one man we could already identify – used the back of the house, so that you couldn't catch the others on film. They knew we were there. The gang must be paying off somebody in the police for information."

"In that case," Clare said, "we'll never catch them."

"That depends."

"On what?"

"They've got another job planned, I'm sure of that. Question is, will they go ahead with it anyway?"

"After this morning?"

"The task force are going back to Birmingham. Presumably the team will find that out. So why not go ahead with the job?"

"You think it's tonight?" Clare asked.

"It's got to be tonight or tomorrow."

"I guess," Clare said, no longer sharing her lover's confidence.

"There's only one problem," Paul went on.

"What?"

"I've no idea where."

12

G ary was about to go to work when Clare got up.
"And where were you last night?" he asked.

"I stayed at Paul's, but didn't get much sleep."

She told him about the abortive raid in West Bridgford.

"Listen," she finished, "I'm meant to be going to a party at Neil's tonight. It's his lodger's birthday and there'll be lots of footballers there. I tried to persuade Paul to go along but he insists he's going to work late, just in case the team do strike somewhere."

"Why's it got anything to do with the Inspector?" Gary asked.

"You should have seen him being interviewed on the early morning Central News," Clare said.

"They did their best to make Paul look a right fool. This case is all getting a bit personal. Anyway, Ruth and Ben are going to the party, too. How about it?"

Gary thought. By this evening he would have spent eight hours with Ben already. He'd been thinking of hitting the clubs, if he had the energy. But he could always go after the party.

"All right," he said. "But just for an hour or so. Why don't Ben and I meet you there?"

"You're on."

There would be several Forest players at the party, he mused. Maybe one of them would remember signing a ball for "Mary".

On Saturday afternoon, as soon as he arrived at work, Gary did something he'd meant to do the day before: checking the police record of Darren Braithwaite. Turned out the boy had been in more trouble than his mate, Joe, and had spent longer in Glen Parva as a result. He'd been convicted of threatening behaviour, breaking and entering and actual bodily harm, all committed before the age of eighteen, which he was now. Next time he got caught, Darren Braithwaite would go away for a long stretch.

Jan Hunt gave the daily orders.

"Gary, let's have you and Ben walking the Maynard Estate, please."

"Oh, come on, Sarge," Gary protested. "That's every day this week. My feet are killing me and we're both going to a party tonight."

"I might let you off tomorrow, then," Jan told him, with a grin.

Ben was late, which was unlike him. Gary called his partner at home. The answering-machine was on. Gary didn't leave a message. He sat in the parade room, pretending to consult his notebook. He liked to look laid back, but actually kept well ahead on his paperwork. Unlike most officers, he didn't have a backlog to get through.

"Aren't we keeping you busy enough?" Paul Grace asked, on the way to his office.

Gary, not wanting to tell tales on Ben, made up a story.

"I'm waiting for a phone call."

The phone on the table rang.

"You'd better answer it then."

A Scots accent asked for Inspector Grace. Gary handed the phone over.

"I see. Yes, thank you. If you could tell me when he leaves, I'd appreciate it." He put the phone down. "That was Glasgow CID. Eddie Broom joined Shirley Wilder this morning. He has his alibi in place."

"Clare said you reckon the team'll do a job tonight," Gary commented.

"It's a possibility."

"Have you got extra men on?"

Paul shook his head. Gary made an offer.

"I'm meant to be going to this party, but I'm not too keen. If you'd like any help, sir…"

"That's good of you, Gary, but you see, it's not my responsibility. I'm helping out as a favour to John Greasby. I'm going to stick around to see if anything happens, but there's no sense in you ruining your weekend."

Jan Hunt came back into the room, interrupting them.

"Hello, sir. Saw you on the news this morning. Why did they interview you, rather than DCI Charlton? It was his cock-up, wasn't it?"

Paul Grace scowled, said nothing, and went through to his office. Jan turned to Gary.

"Someone got out on the wrong side of the bed this morning, didn't they? No Ben yet?"

"Nope. I tried ringing him but…"

"He'll have a good explanation. Want to come out in a car with me? There's a domestic in Hyson Green."

"Beats walking."

"I really ought to go," Ben said. "I'm late already."

"Call in sick."

"I don't like to lie."

"Then tell me the truth. Why?"

Ben shook his head, as though a full explanation was beyond him.

"We've just come back from a brilliant holiday. It was brilliant for you, wasn't it?"

Ben didn't reply. Ruth tried to stop the tears from falling down her cheeks. She had called in on Ben without warning, meaning to catch him before he went off to work. All she'd wanted was to see his face, and make arrangements to meet that evening. Instead, she'd found herself being chucked. Ben got the words out with difficulty. It was as though she'd surprised him into a decision. Something about space and seeing other people.

"There isn't another woman, is there?" she asked, dreading the reply.

"I haven't been with anyone else."

"But you want to get back with Charlene again, is that it?"

Ben's ex was beautiful and intelligent with a prestigious, high-paid job. Ruth had never really understood why he left her.

"No. That's over."

"Then why? I've never put any pressure on you for us to move in together, marry, any of that stuff. We have such a good time…"

"I thought I'd explained."

"All you said was you didn't know what you wanted. But I'm not it, is that what you mean?"

Ben stared out of the window. He was no good at talking about his emotions, Ruth knew that. But, until now, she'd thought that he loved her. For the

126

first few weeks of their relationship, she'd expected a moment like this. She was just some girl he'd picked up on the rebound. But things had gone so well, for so long. She'd let herself get serious about him. More than serious.

"I really ought to get to work," Ben said, standing awkwardly.

"Not until you've explained this to me properly," Ruth raised her voice. "You owe me that much, don't you?"

Ben looked embarrassed by the scene she was making.

"I care for you ... deeply," he said. "But I'm not ready to commit myself to you or anyone else for the rest of my life. We're both too young."

"My mum had been married for three years when she was my age," Ruth argued.

"And now she's miserable and you never call home," Ben argued back. "I've been with two women in my life. I haven't been single since I started university. I want to find out what it's like."

Ruth hated what she was hearing.

"You're leaving me because you want to be single? Because you want one night stands? That's pathetic, Ben. I can tell you what that kind of life's like — empty and lonely. It leaves you feeling disgusting and dead inside. You're leaving me for that?"

"I don't know," Ben said. "I'm not saying it's over for ever, Ruth, but I need some time."

Abruptly, Ruth stood up, nearly knocking her chair over.

"Take all the time in the world. But I won't have you back, Ben Shipman. Not a second time. Don't you think I've got any pride?"

Ben stood, too.

"Ruth, I never wanted to hurt you. It's just…"

She swore at him and walked to the door. When he didn't try to stop her, she reached into her handbag, got out a tissue and her set of keys to his flat. Ruth wiped her eyes, then dropped the keys on the floor and left without looking back.

Her car was parked outside his flat but she walked, too tired and upset to drive. Ruth hadn't slept well, sensing something amiss with Ben. Her last conversation with Charlene Harris kept replaying in her head.

"Let me give you a warning. What he did to me, he'll do to you. Not this week, or next week, but one day. I see it all the time in my job. Once men discover how easy it is to walk away, they do it again, and again."

At the time, Ruth thought that Ben's ex was being cynical. Now it looked like she was right. Charlene knew Ben better than she did. They'd been together for five years, not five months. Maybe Ben already had somebody else lined up. That holiday together, the one she thought had sealed their relationship, was when Ben found out that he was bored with her.

A car hooted and Ruth realized that she was about to walk into traffic. She waited for the Mansfield Road lights to change, not bothering to stop the tears falling down her face. A car pulled up alongside her and she was vaguely aware of the door opening.

"Ruth, are you all right? Ruth?"

Then she was being gently bundled into the back of a squad car.

"We're taking you back to the house," Gary said, putting a comforting arm around her.

"There's no need."

"We were stopping by to see if Ben was ill," Jan told her from the driver's seat. "Have you two had a fight?"

"No. Nothing like that. We've…"

She had trouble getting the words out.

"He chucked me."

"Oh, Ruth…"

Jan and Gary drove her home.

"I'm worried about Paul," Clare was telling Sam.

"You think he's going off you?"

"No. Things are almost too good. In fact, last night, he … never mind. It's this motorway team thing. He's getting obsessed."

Sam laughed.

"Do I hear the pot calling the kettle black? When was it – Easter? – you spent a week watching video tapes on the off-chance that you might spot a single shoplifter?"

"We caught Phoenix as a result."

"And Paul might catch his obsession," Sam pointed out.

"I suppose. But he's talking about working unpaid overtime tonight."

"When he should be at a party with you? Grow up, Clare. You know what's bugging you about Paul? He's too like you. If you're not careful, the pair of you will be in constant competition."

"He'd always win," Clare said. "He's a man, and he's got a degree."

"And can you put up with that?"

Clare thought for a moment.

"I think so, yes."

She considered telling Sam that Paul had asked her to move in with him – or was he offering more than that? But he had said those words in the middle of the night. Maybe she should wait before telling anyone until he'd repeated them, and she'd made her decision.

Her thoughts were interrupted by the sound of the front door opening, closely followed by someone running upstairs.

"Ruth?" Clare called out, recognizing her footsteps.

The lounge door opened. Gary, in uniform, looked in.

"Bad news," he said. "Jan and I were on our way over to see why Ben was late for work. We came across Ruth on Mansfield Road, sobbing her socks off."

"Why?" Clare asked. "Had she been to see Ben? Oh, he hasn't…"

"He has," Gary said.

"Damn," Clare exclaimed. "I'd better go to her now." She ran up the stairs to the top floor. "Ruth, it's me."

She'd locked her door.

"I don't want to talk about it," Ruth called, in a strained voice. "Come back later."

"Are you sure?"

"I'm sure."

Clare went back downstairs. On the street, a horn sounded. Gary was about to leave.

"Jan's outside, waiting. Do you still want me to meet you at this party tonight?"

"I don't know," Clare said. "Could you come home first? I'll meet you here."

"Right you are." He opened the door and signalled to Jan that he was coming. "Look after Ruth. She seems pretty broken up."

"I will."

But Clare could do nothing until Ruth was ready to talk. What had happened scared her. She hadn't seen it coming and nor, she was sure, had Ruth.

Ruth had confided in Clare. She'd dreamt of a future with Ben: house, garden, babies. A selfish thought clouded Clare's mind: if Ruth and Ben could fall apart so easily, if her parents could call it a day after twenty-two years, what chance was there for her and Paul?

Ben was in the parade room doing paperwork when Gary and Jan got in.

"Sorry, Sarge," he offered. "I had some personal business."

"We know," Jan told Ben, confusing him.

"What do you—?"

"I want you and Gary out walking, now."

"You're the boss."

Gary and Ben set off. The Meadows area was quiet today. Football fans had to walk through there to get to both grounds, but Forest were playing away, while County's tiny gate rarely gave any bother these days.

"We came looking for you," Gary told his partner. "Found Ruth instead."

"Oh. She told you, then?"

"She told us."

"I feel a complete bastard."

"What happened?" Gary asked. "Was she playing away?"

"Of course not."

"You, then?"

"I've been tempted," Ben admitted. "We were getting into a bit of a rut."

Gary shook his head. He liked Ruth. "Some folk don't know when they're lucky," he said.

"The longer I left it," Ben protested, "the worse it would have been."

"I guess," Gary said. "When did you make up your mind?"

"Yesterday."

"Did it have something to do with the holiday?"

Ben looked at him. Gary had, he realized, tried to get in too close again. Men like Ben only had these conversations after several pints. Or not, since Ben didn't drink much.

"Ever been with someone – you know, I mean *been with* someone – but found yourself thinking about someone else?" Ben asked.

"Yeah."

"That's why I had to finish with her."

Gary nearly asked the next question: *And what about the someone else?* But Ben's manner told him that he'd got as close as he was going to get today. They were walking past the Wilder house.

"Think I'll pop in," Ben said, "see if Julie or Curt can give us something."

"Do you really think that, if they knew something, they'd tell you?"

"I got something yesterday," Ben told him.

"From Julie? I heard. 'S funny," Gary said. "She doesn't strike me as a grass."

Ben looked embarrassed. "People don't always realize that what they're telling you is useful. Look, I'll meet you at the old people's home in fifteen minutes or so, all right?" The two of them tried to look in on the home a couple of times a week, have a cup of tea. The visit had nothing to do with detection or preventative policing, and everything to do with reassuring the residents.

"Whatever you say," Gary told him. "Good luck."

"You find it?" Joe asked Darren.

They were back at the squat which, despite the auction, hadn't been sold.

"No. It's gone."

"If I'd known it was here in the first place..." Joe complained.

"I told you. It's Rob's."

"He's not going to need it where he is."

Joe knew Rob Wardle from school and from Glen Parva, where their stay had overlapped by a couple of weeks. In both places, he'd steered well clear of him. Rob was bad news – the sort of bloke who'd strangle a cat for fun, then throw the body into a school playground and enjoy the kids' screams. It worried Joe that Darren seemed to look up to him.

"How long's he got to go now?" Joe asked.

"Not long."

134

Would Darren hook up with Rob when he got out? Maybe it would be good riddance. Joe was fed up with his sidekick. If Joe dumped Darren, Dean might be more pally with him. But who was he kidding? Dean would never talk to him again after the stunt that they were going to pull tomorrow. And it was all Darren's fault.

It was Darren who had talked Joe into blackmailing Dean. Joe, angry that his friend didn't want to know him any more, went along with it. Now there was no going back. Or was there? He hadn't gone through with it yet. Joe hadn't done anything that the police could put him away for.

"I'm going for a walk," he told Darren. "Meet you back at the car in half an hour." Without waiting for a reply, Joe walked to the Wilder house. He would have another go at asking Julie out. He had a new idea. If he didn't do the burglary tomorrow night, if he got back in with Dean, then he would have the perfect opportunity. He could invite Julie to Dean's party tomorrow. Half the Forest team would be there. It was perfect.

Yes! After all, why not? Drop Darren, kick the burglary into touch, tell Dean he was off the hook, then take Julie to the party? She couldn't turn down an offer like that. True, Joe had hardly any money and nowhere to live. But those were minor difficulties. He turned into Julie's street, his heart starting to lift.

A black policeman was knocking on the Wilders' front door. Seeing him, Joe's bubble deflated. Who was he trying to kid? There'd always be the police, wherever he turned. The only life for a bloke like him was crime. It was the only life for a woman like Julie, too. He'd burgle Umberto and burgle him big. He'd come back for Julie with money in his pocket and a big car outside her house. That was the way to win her.

"Oh," Julie said. "Here you are again."

"I can't keep away," Ben told her, playfully.

Promising, Julie thought. "Come in," she said. "I was just making some tea."

He probably wanted information. Julie had felt bad, the other day, telling Ben about Mum and Eddie. Not that there was anything to it. They were just on a little holiday. But she had a crush on Ben, and the policeman was exploiting it. Maybe he also fancied her a bit. Julie wanted to think so. She was happy to give him any excuse to visit.

After all, who else was interested in her? That lad, Joe, who Curt brought round, had managed to get himself evicted. And Ben was there, in charge. Imagine the humiliation if she'd been with Joe at the time! Luckily the Mansfield lad hadn't seen Julie watching, so hadn't let on that he knew her. And Julie, relieved, had blurted out a silly comment to Ben. She couldn't remember what it was now –

something about being alone tonight. He'd probably interpreted it as *you can have me any time*.

Trouble was, that was exactly what she meant … in a way. There was a song Mum used to play before the CD player got stolen: "*'Cause Cheap is How I Feel*". That was how Julie felt, in a room alone with Ben Shipman: out of her league and grateful for whatever crumbs of company he gave her.

"I haven't got any more information for you," she said, taking in the two mugs.

"I wasn't after any." Ben sat on the sofa looking awkward, even a little embarrassed. "Actually, I was wondering what you were doing later on."

"Me?"

He smiled. "Yeah, after what you said I thought … well, it's not much fun being alone in the house on a Saturday night."

"No," Julie said. "It's not."

"I get off at ten," Ben told her, "and I've got nothing on. We could rent a video, order a pizza…"

Julie was tongue-tied. She didn't know how to accept, not without gushing or sounding all girly. This was a daydream coming true.

"Just say if you don't want to. I mean, no strings or anything…"

Julie relaxed a bit. "No. That'd be fine. Just after ten then?"

"I'll look forward to it. Now I'd better be going. My partner…"

He couldn't get out of the house quickly enough. Julie thought about his words: *no strings*. That meant he wanted a one night stand. His girlfriend would be away for the weekend and Julie was a quick bit on the side. Could she put up with that?

Julie wasn't cheap. She'd only been with two blokes in her life and she'd never stolen another woman's man. But she wanted Ben badly, even if it was only for one night.

No. That wasn't right. She wanted him, not just for one night but for companionship; love, even. When Julie was with Ben, she felt better about herself. She would make that clear when he came round: conversation and a cuddle, that was all he would get. Then maybe, just maybe, he would come back for more.

Julie pinched herself. Who was she kidding? If Ben Shipman asked her to jump into the Trent for him, she'd do it.

13

"You ought to go to the party," Clare said. "It'll take your mind off things."

"No way," Ruth said. "Ben might be there."

"Believe me," Clare said. "Ben won't show his face at anywhere you might be for quite some time."

"But he's Neil's best friend. He has to be there."

"It's not Neil's party. It's his lodger's."

"So why on earth should we go?" Ruth asked.

"Because Neil asked."

"He asked you. To show off."

Clare knew that Ruth was right, but didn't want to leave her alone on a Saturday night.

"Come on. I might be able to set you up with a sexy footballer. You like football more than I do. They say that Umberto Capricio's coming, and he's single."

"I don't think so," Ruth said. "You go. I'll have an early night."

"I can't leave you on your own."

"I won't be alone. Sam'll look after me. Maybe we'll even go for a drink."

"I really don't want to go," Clare said. "But I promised Neil. He kept on about it."

"Fine," Ruth said. "Don't be guilty. Go."

But Clare did feel guilty. The three women watched TV and shared a large bottle of wine. Ruth didn't want to talk. That much was clear. Clare was relieved when ten o'clock went by and Gary came home.

"Give me five minutes to get changed," he said.

As usual, Gary's five minutes took nearly half an hour. After twenty minutes, Clare called a taxi. It was only a fifteen-minute walk but Clare didn't want to be walking through Forest Fields in a low cut dress at this time of night. Before the couple left, Ruth went to bed, saying she was exhausted.

"Thanks for coming with me," Clare told Gary when they were in the taxi. "We don't have to stay long."

"You never know," Gary told her. "It might be fun."

"You never know," Clare agreed.

She wondered how Paul was getting on.

Neil and Dean sat in Neil's front room, using the edges of the armchairs, cans in hand. In the kitchen,

Melanie was pretending to prepare snack food with a girl called Karen, who was Dean's date for the evening. The food had been ready for ages, but the two girls wanted to gossip away from the men. Nevertheless, Neil could hear them over the music.

"I can't believe I'm here," Karen was saying, "meeting players from the Forest team. Imagine, Umberto's coming! Have you met him?"

"You'd better watch out," Neil told Dean. "Your date sounds like she's more interested in Capricio than in you."

"She won't have any luck with Umberto," Dean mumbled, glancing irritably at the clock. "Where is everybody?"

"Paul and Ben don't get off work until ten," Neil said. "And the players are probably celebrating today's victory in the pub, aren't they?"

"I guess. But I hope they show up before throwing out time."

A car pulled up outside. A taxi. Neil made out the familiar figure of the former European player of the year. He hoped that Umberto wouldn't be embarrassed by being the first proper guest to arrive. As the doorbell rang, a second taxi stopped.

"I can't stay long," Neil heard Umberto tell Dean. "But I thought…"

"Hi, everyone."

"Clare!" Neil said. "Good of you to come. And … eh…"

"This is Gary. Paul's doing an extra shift, so I thought…"

"You're very welcome."

Neil turned to see if Dean was getting drinks, but the youth was on the phone.

"What can I get you? Umberto, this is Clare…"

"Oh, yes, your father is Italian, I believe."

"That's me."

Umberto began speaking to Clare in Italian. Gary looked on, bemused. Clare's Italian wasn't strong, Neil knew, but she appeared to understand Umberto. Anyway, she was smiling a lot. The doorbell rang again and Neil decided to let people get their own drinks from now on. As Dean put the phone down, half the Forest first team filled Neil's small living-room. This was going to be a night to remember.

Joe clicked the mobile phone off and walked along the footbridge across the river. Evidently Umberto had said that he wouldn't stay at the party for long, but Dean promised to give Joe another ring when he left. There was plenty of time. Darren was waiting near the house, keeping an eye out for trouble. They'd parked the car on Balmoral Avenue, a short walk from Umberto's. Parking was tight in these parts and Joe needed to be sure they had a space. A local might spot the stolen car without the resident's permit, but it didn't matter. Once they'd hidden the stuff in the hut, they'd dump the car somewhere, set it on fire.

Joe wondered what the Italian footballer's home would be like. This was the biggest place he'd ever had a go at. He'd been surprised that Dean had done as he asked: wangled an invite to the house, mapped out the lay-out, even damaged a window for them. It showed how scared he was of people finding out his past. It had nothing to do with friendship. Dean's friendship had always meant a lot to Joe. But the footballer had no time for his old friend now. Joe was tempted to call the *Evening Post* tomorrow, spill the beans on Dean's criminal past. But they used to be best mates, and he'd made a promise.

Darren was waiting by the river, just in view of the house.

"All clear?"

"No problems. A few drunken kids on the river bank. That's the lot."

"All right. Stick to the plan. I'll let you in by the back door, but don't come until you see a light in there."

Darren was slow. He needed everything repeating. He was also big, which was why Joe was the one climbing in through the downstairs toilet window. Dean had broken the lock on it, making entry easy, but, still, this was the most dangerous part, the one where he might make a lot of noise and wake the woman upstairs. Or Dean might have given them the wrong information. If the burglar alarm was switched on, then, the moment Joe came out of the toilet, it would sound, and he would have to run like hell.

But there was no sound, bar the muffled noise as glass broke on to adhesive tape. Then Joe was inside, ready to start the largest haul of his short criminal career.

Paul Grace was bored. Eleven o'clock had come and gone. Officially, he no longer had a role to play. Another Inspector was in charge of this shift and five others. Paul could be with Clare now. Dancing maybe. Clare liked to dance. Instead, he was listening to the radio, trying to hunt out traces of activity which might hint at the motorway team. The team were most likely to strike in the next hour. Half eleven was their preferred time. Only trouble was, the crimes were never reported for another hour and sometimes not until the following morning.

Paul couldn't wait any longer. He'd go out in a squad car, listen to the radio in that. The team were most likely to strike in one of the well-heeled parts of the city, which meant the Park, Mapperley Park, parts of West Bridgford or one of the outlying villages. If Paul was in a car when the call came, he would get there quicker.

He took an unmarked Sierra out and set off

through the Meadows. This time next week, he'd be in Paris with Clare, in the shadow of the Eiffel Tower. The money for the trip had come from a casino win. Paul was tempted to go to the casino now, abandon this wild-goose chase. But he was trying to stay away from them. Saturday wasn't his favourite night at the tables anyway: too many drunken amateurs, messing up the action. More importantly, Clare disapproved. She wanted him to give up gambling. He thought that she was wrong. There was no harm in it. Maybe he would try to stop anyway. For her.

Going after the motorway team was the biggest gamble of Paul's career. If he won, the sky was the limit. Lose, and promotion would be a long time coming. He drove across the Trent, looking over at the expensive houses which lined the river, wondering if, one day, he'd be able to afford one of them.

Paul turned down Radcliffe Road, driving away from the city, out past the house that the team had been using as its base. Now that the hide-out was no use, where would they go to divide their takings? Did these men have homes? They were like ghosts. Sometimes, Paul wondered if the motorway team really existed. Wouldn't it be ironic if they turned out to be several different sets of crooks, all using the same *modus operandi*?

At first it seemed that they had all the time in the

world. While Darren disconnected stereo equipment, Joe sneaked upstairs, where he assured himself that Mrs Capricio was sleeping soundly, and
relieved her of her jewellery box, which she kept on
a bedside table. He unplugged her bedside phone,
then went to the footballer's bedroom, where he
found a spare credit card, some English and Italian
cash, and a bunch of gold jewellery. He took a few
shirts from the wardrobe, where he also found a
sports bag to put all the stuff into. He hid the
money in his underpants, not wanting to share it
with Darren.

His partner was still in the living-room. Posters
and prints were strewn across the floor.

"I can't find a safe," he told Joe.

"I don't think there is one," Joe replied, opening
the bag to reveal his haul. "Look at this lot I got
upstairs."

"Ace. You want some of these CDs?"

"Why not?"

Without sorting them, Darren began to throw the
CDs into the bag on top of the jewellery.

"Hold on!"

Joe stuffed a couple of Umberto's shirts from the
other bag on top of the jewellery to stop the gold
getting scratched. They'd been in the house for less
than twenty minutes. There was still plenty of time
to take whatever else they could get their hands on.

"I'll take the first lot to the car," Darren said.

"Make sure everything's cool outside." He left through the kitchen door, the way that Joe had let him in. Joe had a quick look at the locked room, where the footballer kept his valuable paintings. You'd need a crowbar to get into it and they didn't have one. Anyway, what would Joe do with paintings? He checked the drinks cabinet. Nothing fancy – the Italian wasn't a big boozer. There was a lot of wine in the kitchen, but Joe didn't drink wine.

Then something funny happened. The front doorbell rang. Joe nearly didn't answer it. Umberto was out, and would hardly ring his own front doorbell. Maybe it was some drunk who had decided to pester the player. More probably it was Darren, pratting about. The doorbell rang again, a double ring this time. It was bound to be Darren. What if he woke up the old woman upstairs? The guy was a nutter, untrustworthy. It was time Joe dumped him. Angrily, he went to answer it.

"If this is your idea of a joke…" Joe said, as he pulled the door open. Then he stopped. Two masked men pushed their way into the house. One of them pinned Joe against the wall while the other closed the door.

"Who the hell are you?" asked Joe's captor.

The party was small, but pretty good, as parties went. Neil enjoyed talking to the Forest players, except for Umberto Capricio, who Clare had monopolized for most of the evening. Dean seemed ill at ease with the other members of the team. Neil wasn't sure why. They seemed to like him well enough. There was much good-natured teasing about who he would be substituted for next and whether he'd start the game for the second leg cup tie against County on Tuesday.

Neil didn't let on that he was a County supporter. It seemed rude, somehow. Anyway, he'd already almost given up on the game. Forest were all over County in the first leg, at Meadow Lane, and were unlucky to only win by the single goal. The whole idea behind these two-legged games in the early stages of the cup was to give lower league sides the experience of playing at home against the big boys. Well, County had had their learning experience. On Tuesday, they were likely to be thrashed.

"So, when's my lodger going to get a regular place in the first team?" Neil asked the captain, who smiled indulgently.

"The manager's breaking him in slowly. You've got to watch players at his age. There's so many I remember who were wonderful at eighteen or nineteen, but then they got their first big injury, or made a bad transfer decision. Next thing you know, they're sinking like a stone to the lower divisions. Dean's got plenty of time on his side."

"I've got to go," Clare interrupted. It was nearly twelve. "Will you call me a taxi?"

"But you've only been here an hour."

"An hour and a half," Clare said. "It's been fun."

"But we've hardly talked," Neil protested. "I know Melanie wanted to get to know you."

Clare shook her head. "You don't want the two of us comparing notes, Neil. Believe me. She seems nice though. I'm glad you're happy."

Neil called for a taxi. In the kitchen, Dean was snogging Karen and Melanie was talking to the Forest keeper. It was all right, Neil told himself, the player was wearing a wedding ring. Gary had given up asking the older players whether they remembered signing a football five years before and had started talking to Umberto about the Italian club scene. Neil went back to join Clare, but she was nowhere to be seen.

"So you're a policeman?" one of the reserves asked Neil.

"Yes. I'm in CID…"

He was still explaining when the taxi pulled up outside. Out of the corner of his eye, Neil had seen Clare come down from the toilet. Now he saw her in the kitchen and was shocked. Umberto Capricio had his arm around her. He was playing with one of the straps which held up her dress, but had fallen loose on to her shoulder. Gary was standing with them, laughing at some joke the Italian Romeo had just told.

"Clare!" Neil called. "Your taxi's here."

"Thanks."

It wasn't just Clare leaving. It was Gary and Umberto, too.

"Many thanks," Capricio said, shaking Neil's hand at the door. "I had a good time. Say goodbye to Dean for me. He seems … preoccupied."

Then they were off, with Gary in the front seat, Umberto and Clare in the back. Neil felt unreasonably jealous.

Suddenly, everyone seemed to be leaving. As the players said goodnight, Dean broke away from Karen to play the host.

"Where's Umberto?" he asked Neil.

"Left ten minutes ago."

Dean swore, then tried to explain. "I was meant to phone for a taxi." He hurried to the phone. The expression on his face wasn't that of someone calling a taxi. After a minute, he put the phone down without speaking.

"I hope your policeman friend finds out who this Mary was," the captain told Dean, as he left with two other players. They were going on to a club.

"What was that about?" Dean asked Neil, when they'd gone. "The Mary thing?"

Neil explained. "Gary found this football which two toerags from Mansfield had thieved, signed by all the Forest team of five years ago. He knows they nicked it, but not who from. If he finds out who, then the woman can have her ball back, and he can put them away."

Dean's face went white.

"They lied to me," he said.

"Who lied to you?"

"Mary, my landlady. She had a signed ball. It was gone. I never noticed, but now I'm sure – it was gone. Don't you see? It was them, they killed her, or good as."

Neil cursed himself for a fool. He'd never connected the ball with Mary up the road. He'd expected it to have belonged to a young girl.

"Do you mean the lads from Mansfield that Gary was on about?" he asked Dean.

Dean nodded. Tears were forming in his eyes. "You met them yesterday – Darren and Joe."

"The burglars were *friends of yours*?"

"Joe used to be."

"I don't suppose you know where they're living, by any chance?"

Dean put his head in his hands. He looked as though he was trying to make up his mind about something. Finally, he spoke.

"I don't know where they're living, but I know where they are now – burgling Umberto's house. I just rang them to say that he's on the way home."

Neil tried to take all this in. Dean was in it up to his ears, that much was clear.

"So they'll have left by now?"

"I don't know," Dean said. "You see, no one answered the call."

Neil picked up the phone, dialled the police number and asked to be put through to Inspector Grace, urgently.

Paul Grace was driving around the Maynard Estate. He looked at his watch. Ten to twelve. If the team were doing a job, they would have just gone in. The way they worked, they emptied the house, then took one of the house's occupants with them to a nearby cash machine, leaving the rest of the household tied up. At the cash machine, they drew out two lots of money on each card – just before and just after midnight so they could get twice the maximum daily amount. Then they disappeared into the night, dumping their prisoner on the way.

A message came in on his radio.

"It's Neil Foster here, sir. I've just had information that two youths are in the process of burgling Umberto Capricio's house. The footballer left a party at my place ten minutes ago. He's going to arrive home any time now. Clare said you were pulling an extra shift tonight, so I thought I'd get straight on to you."

Paul got the address, then asked, "Have you called anyone else?"

"No. I thought—"

"All right. Leave it with me. Thanks, Neil."

Paul called it in himself and set off towards Trent bridge. What if news came in about the motorway team while he was following up this small burglary? No point in worrying about it. He'd been chasing rainbows.

Paul turned on to the street where the footballer lived. There was nowhere to park, but that didn't matter. He wanted to block the street off. As Paul got out of the car, he tried to decide whether to go in, or wait for back-up. Had Umberto's taxi already been and gone?

There was a light on in the hallway, implying that somebody was home. Then Paul spotted him. The man was sitting in a car parked halfway down the street, and he was eyeing Paul nervously. He wasn't a youth, but could he be the burglars' getaway driver? Either way, Paul decided, he wanted a word with him.

He walked over to the car, a large saloon, and rapped on the window. The man frowned, and pulled his window down. Paul stared at him, memorizing his face, and making a connection. This man looked very like one of the men he had seen with Eddie Broom last Sunday afternoon. It was probably a co-incidence. Paul kept recognizing members of the motorway team in every new face he saw.

"Seen a man getting out of a taxi in the last few minutes?" he asked.

"Ain't seen nothing, mate."

A Brummie accent.

"How long have you been out here?"

"Not long. I was just going off to pick my daughter up from a party. You're blocking me in, as it happens. Think you could move that?"

"Shortly. Excuse me."

The squad car which Paul had called stopped at the end of the road, next to his vehicle. He ran over to fill them in on what was going on.

"They might still be in there. I think that bloke is the driver. Take him in." But, as the officers hurried back to the car, Paul saw that the saloon door was open. He could hear frantic footsteps, heading towards the river bank.

"After him! I'll cover the house."

The burglars wouldn't get far without their getaway driver. But maybe Paul should go back to his car, call for more back-up. He approached the house, checking to see what was going on. The front door was closed, but, when he tried it, swung open easily. No one left their front door unlocked in this day and age. Paul walked in. One of the other officers would be behind him in a minute, but he wished he had a personal radio, not just the one in the car. Then he heard a voice.

"Here he is."

The door at the end of the hallway opened.

"Freeze!"

A man in a dark mask was pointing a gun at him.

14

The way it had happened was like this: one of the masked men pushed Joe back into the hall-way. There were two of them, and they were waving guns around. The one who hadn't spoken pushed his way past Joe and walked into the living-room.

"Where's Umberto?" the first one in asked.

"At a party. He's not back yet."

"So who are you? The lodger?"

From the front room, Joe could hear the other one swearing.

"I'm—"

The other one came back out of the living-room.

"This place has already been cleaned out."

Now the first one started swearing. He pushed Joe into the dining-room, looked at the chaos that the two burglars had created. Darren still wasn't back from the car. It occurred to Joe that Darren might have double-crossed him, cleared off with all the stuff while Joe looked around for leftovers.

"Where's the money?" the first one asked. "Give us the money, now."

Joe wasn't in a mood to argue. Not with a gun poking into his stomach. He reached into his underpants and pulled it all out.

"This is everything," he said.

"*Everything!* Did you find the safe?"

"I don't think there is a safe," Joe told him, "not unless it's upstairs. I didn't look too hard up there."

Thief number one called to thief number two.

"Upstairs. There's got to be a safe."

"You'd better watch out," Joe said. "There's an old lady asleep in the first bedroom. I disconnected her phone, but..."

Thief number two nodded and kept on.

"Look," Joe told thief number one, "you've got the money. Let me go now. I wouldn't have done this place if I'd known you were coming in, too. You're out of my league. I'm being straight with you."

"I'm sure you are," his captor said, voice heavy with sarcasm. "Have you had the paintings?"

"I didn't even get into the room."

"Sit down."

When Joe had done as he was told, thief number

one put down his gun, then took the big rucksack from his back and emptied it. Out rolled several long cardboard tubes of the kind used to deliver posters or paintings. There was also a crowbar. Thief number one pointed at the door to the locked room.

"Get to work," he told Joe.

Joe was just setting to the door when the phone in his pocket rang. Automatically, he reached for it.

"Don't answer it," the thief said. Then he added, in a mocking tone, "You always take a mobile on a job, do you?"

Joe decided it was safest to square with him.

"I've got this mate. He's meant to ring me when Umberto's on his way home."

"You're cleverer than you look. How far away is he?"

"Ten, fifteen minutes."

Thief number two came in.

"No safe upstairs. This lad seems to have cleared out the jewellery. There's nothing left worth having."

"Where's the jewellery?" number one asked Joe.

"In the car."

"Which is where?"

"Balmoral Avenue, just along the river."

"Describe it."

Joe did. Thief number one turned to his accomplice.

"Get out quick. Tell Kev there's a short delay.

We're waiting for the footballer to get home. Then check this car out. Get the good stuff." He turned back to Joe. "Anyone in it?"

"No," Joe lied. "It's open."

He didn't know why he lied. Habit, probably. To protect Darren, maybe, if his friend hadn't already double-crossed him, cleared off. Darren wanted to bring his friend Rob, just out of nick, on this job. He'd been pissed off when Joe said he didn't trust Rob. What if Darren had decided to work with Rob in future? Joe decided that he didn't care. It was Darren who'd followed Dean home, found out where he lived. It was Darren who talked Joe into putting pressure on Dean to help them get into Capricio's. Joe had messed up a friendship for one measly burglary. If Darren had done a runner, Joe would get him back.

He lifted the crowbar to do as he'd been told.

"Sit down," thief number one ordered now. "No point in breaking into the paintings room, waking up the whole street. We'll let that nice Mr Capricio open it for us, then take him on a ride to the cash machine. If you're lucky, we might take you with us."

Two minutes later, thief number two returned.

"Well…?"

"I couldn't find the car."

Number one glared at Joe.

"I left it there, I swear."

"He might be telling the truth, Chris. I get all these streets muddled in the dark, and there are people around, coming out of the pubs. I had to take my mask off." The narrow cut-out eyes of the man called Chris, the man who was clearly the boss, glared at him.

"Sorry."

Joe knew what that was about. They weren't meant to use first names, but now he knew two of them: Chris and Kev. Would they kill him for this knowledge?

"I'm not happy," number two said. "All these people around. A cul-de-sac. We're too exposed. We should have stuck to the isolated places."

"This is the last job," Chris hissed. "We agreed. Those paintings are our pension plan." He turned to Joe. "If we let you live," he said, "you saw nothing, know nothing. No – even better, if the police catch you, you confess everything. Show them the stuff you got in the car and say you threw the paintings in the Trent. Understood?"

Joe nodded. "Who shall I say was with me?"

"I don't give a—"

The other one shushed him. All three of them listened carefully. It sounded like Umberto Capricio was back.

"Here he is," thief number two said.

Thief number one, Chris, lifted his gun and kicked open the door to the hall.

"Freeze!"

"I'm a police officer," Paul told the man with the gun. "This street is blocked off by my officers."

"Bollocks."

"Drop your weapon. You do not have to—"

"Forget it. Inside. *Now*."

The man in the mask pushed past Paul and went to the front door. This wasn't a couple of young thugs, Paul realized. This was the motorway team. Paul prayed that he survived to arrest them. The masked man came back.

"Car's empty."

"Now do you believe me?" Paul asked. "You can forget your driver. We've arrested him." He hoped that this was true. "If you drop that gun now, I'll forget that you pointed it at me. You're not known for violence. I respect that."

The man pushed him through to the living-room. There was a second one in there, also wearing a mask. There was also a third person, a scared-looking teenager. He must be one of the kids who Neil had called about.

"We've got to get out," the first one said.

There was a noise at the door, followed by the voice of one of the officers from the patrol car. "Inspector?"

"Come on," the second one said to the youth. "Take us to your car."

"What about the paintings?" the first one said.

"They're no use in the nick. Come on. Do him."

For a moment, Paul thought that the masked man was going to shoot him. He saw the man's eyes as he approached and was sure which he was: the balding one who seemed to be in charge. He was taller than the other one. Paul would be able to identify him later. The bald man clobbered Paul on the side of the face with the butt of his gun.

"Come after us," he threatened, "and you get the other side of this."

A moment later they were gone and a uniformed officer was in the room with him.

"We got him, sir. What happened here?"

"Get the armed response unit," Paul croaked. "Two men in masks, with at least one gun. And call as many cars here as we can manage. If we seal off the area quickly, we might get them both."

He meant to explain about the youth, and the other getaway car, but as the officer spoke into his radio, Paul lost consciousness.

Joe looked up and down Balmoral Avenue, fearing for his life, "I'm sorry," he told the two men. "It's not here."

"How the hell can that be?"

There was no point in lying, Joe got ready to beg.

"I was with a mate. I think he scarpered when he saw you, or when he heard the police coming, I don't know…"

Chris cocked the gun. "I ought to—"

"Steady," the other one said. "What good will that do?"

The two men glanced at each other. Police sirens were sounding in the distance. Someone was walking over the footbridge, singing to himself. "*Got a black magic woman, got a black magic woman...*" Joe considered making a run for it. In films, you saw blokes running in a zigzag to avoid getting shot. Did that work? Probably not. But he might just avoid getting killed. Joe didn't want to die. He glanced over Chris's shoulder.

"Don't even think about it," Chris said.

Joe felt the gun press against his chest. "Someone's coming," the other bloke said.

"Better take the mask off," Chris told him. He pulled off his own ski mask to reveal a balding head and angry eyes. The other did the same. They were both older than Joe would have thought, less hard-looking. Chris pointed the gun back at him and Joe realized that he'd missed his chance to run. He needed to bargain instead

"I can show you a quick way out of here," Joe offered. "Over the footbridge."

Chris looked at the other one. "What do you reckon?"

"If they catch us running away, that's as good as admitting guilt."

"We didn't get anything," Chris said. "I'm not

162

going down for this."

"We could dump the hats and gun in the river…"

Without further discussion, they began to walk towards the Trent. Chris put one hand on Joe's back, pulling him along with them. "Brazen it out, yeah… They'll pick us up, but a good brief'll get us sorted, no trouble."

"They've no prints, no witnesses, except…"

He looked at Joe. Both men were nervous now and, perhaps, trigger happy… The sirens got nearer. The man from the footbridge stopped singing as he saw them. He walked by the three of them without glancing in their direction. As soon as he was past them, Chris began wrapping the woollen masks around the gun. Was he doing that to muffle the sound or…?

"They'll hear," the other one side.

"I know," Chris told him.

The guy who'd walked past began to sing again. "*Got a black magic woman and she's trying to make a devil out of me.*"

Chris turned to Joe. "You didn't see us. Right, son? Because if you ever…"

He didn't need to finish the threat, because Joe was crying. He felt something damp on his leg and realized that he'd wet himself, too. Chris looked down, laughed, then stretched back his arm and threw the weapon into the middle of the river.

"Go on," he told Joe, "get lost."

"Right," Joe said, then ran like the blazes before they had the chance to change their minds. As he reached the bridge he could hear yet more sirens, and megaphones, urging the fugitives to give themselves up. But there was no one waiting at the other end of the footbridge. He'd had a lucky escape, Joe knew that. But if he ever got his hands on Darren, he'd kill him.

Neil crossed Trent bridge only to find the right-hand side of Loughborough Road blocked off beyond County Hall. He paid the taxi driver and ran towards Umberto's street. Armed police units were getting into position. People were being pulled off the paths into police vans. All this for two toerags from Mansfield? As Neil walked down the road, Paul Grace staggered out of Umberto Capricio's house, a uniformed officer trying to help him along.

"What happened?" Neil asked the Inspector, whose head was bleeding.

"The motorway team. They were after the footballer's paintings – must have bumped into your burglars when they were about it."

"Did you catch them?"

"Only the driver. The other two got away."

A uniform interrupted them.

"Sir, we've picked a couple of men up by the river, just off Balmoral Avenue. No masks or guns, but they might be our men: early forties, one of them without much hair."

"I'm on my way," Grace said, beckoning Neil. "Come on. This is thanks to you."

There were two men standing in the back of a police van. "What *is* going on?" the tall, bald one said. "A riot? I was just going about my business…"

Then he saw Paul and shut up.

"That's them," the Inspector said. "I recognize this man's voice – he's the one who assaulted me. Arrest them."

"Congratulations, sir," Neil said as the van drove away. "And now I think we'd better get you to Casualty."

"Just take me to Clare," Grace said, his voice unnaturally high. He was in shock, Neil guessed, from being hit over the head. "Clare will look after me."

"Casualty first," Neil said, taking the Inspector to an ambulance.

"One thing puzzles me," Paul Grace said, as his head was being bandaged.

"What's that, sir?"

"Why didn't the footballer come home?"

Neil hesitated. He didn't want to ruin the Inspector's evening. But nor did he want to lie.

"I'm missing something, aren't I?" Paul Grace said, rubbing his head. "Tell me what it is, Neil."

"There's probably nothing in it."

"What? Tell me."

"It's just that ... Umberto left the party with Clare, sir."

Grace stared at Neil, triumph fading from his face. Then he buried his head in his hands.

15

Joe ran. He didn't know where to go. Darren was hiding somewhere with the stuff. But where would the bastard be? Joe had worked out the real reason why the two masked men had let him go – they wanted to pin the burglary on him. But, he remembered, the policeman had seen all three of them. He had also seen Joe's face, which was bad. Though at least it meant he knew Joe wasn't the one who hit him.

Only question was, who called the police?

Joe was a fugitive now. He was bound to be identified, even if Dean hadn't coughed, which Joe doubted. Where to go? There was no way to get back to the hut without taking a taxi, which was too dangerous – the driver might remember him. The squat he'd just been thrown out of was also out of the question. Joe only knew one person on the Maynard Estate who might put him up, Curt Wilder. Joe had only befriended Curt because he wanted to get off with Julie, but Curt wasn't to know that. Maybe he'd help.

Joe would really show himself up tonight, arriving at Julie's house in soiled trousers. But what alternative was there? He hurried to the house and knocked on the door. There was a light on in the front room. He could hear the TV. It sounded like Curt was in.

The front door opened on to the living-room. Julie Wilder answered his knock. Despite the state he was in, Joe took a good look at her. Julie was wearing a smart blouse and a short skirt. Her face was made up, the lipstick slightly smudged. She looked fantastic.

"What is it?" she asked. "Do you know what time it is?"

"I'm sorry," Joe said. "I've come to see Curt."

"He's not here," Julie told him. "He's staying over at his girlfriend's."

Joe didn't look into Julie's eyes, but over her shoulder. There was a bloke sitting on the sofa, wine glass in his hand. Joe couldn't make out his face.

"Thing is, I'm in a bit of bother. Need a place to kip."

Julie was firm. "If Curt was here I'd let you stay, but I don't really know you, Joe, and I've got company. Sorry."

"'S all right."

As she shut the door, Joe could hear Julie telling her boyfriend, "Just a friend of Curt's". Then he began to run again, taking side streets into the city. Joe didn't know Nottingham that well, but remembered that there were some small caves at the bottom of the Lace Market. Tramps and crusties used them to crash in sometimes. Maybe he'd be lucky, find a blanket or sleeping bag that someone had left behind. Tomorrow, he'd find Darren.

"I'd better get going," Umberto said, at two in the morning. "I don't like my mother to wake and find I'm not home."

"Doesn't it cramp your style, living with your mother?"

"It's only for a few months of the year," Umberto said, starting to dress. "And you're the first person I've been with for … oh, a long time."

"Will I see you again?"

"Do you want to?"

"You know I do."

"I'd like it, but … we have to be discreet."

"I'll second that. No reason why anyone has to know we're more than friends."

"You work shifts?" Umberto asked.

"Nights this week, but not starting until Wednesday."

"Maybe I could see you after the game on Tuesday. You want a couple of tickets?"

"No, ta. I hate football. But we could meet…"

"Come to my place. After my mother's asleep. About ten, say. I'll cook you supper."

"No need for supper."

"I always like to eat after a match. Let me cook. You can tell me how my cooking compares to Clare's."

"She was brilliant tonight, making it look like you two were leaving together."

Umberto smiled.

"My reputation with the other players is safe."

Gary returned the grin. "Wouldn't you prefer to be out of the closet?"

"Here? Maybe it's possible. But in Italy? I'd never play for my country again. I've got to go."

The two men kissed. Gary stroked the footballer's thick, curly hair.

"See you on Tuesday."

Then he was gone. Gary, for the third or fourth time that evening, pinched himself, unable to believe his luck.

"Time you were going," Julie said, keeping her voice playful so that he wouldn't be able to tell how serious she was. The film had finished long ago and the wine was all gone. They'd spent the last hour fooling around, but now was decision time. Julie was tired and didn't want to do something she'd regret. Though most people, she'd heard, regretted the things they hadn't done, not the ones they had.

"Can't I stay the night?" Ben asked, softly.

"You don't want to wake up on the Maynard Estate," Julie said, teasingly. "Everyone will know what you've been up to."

"It wasn't waking up I was thinking about," he said, caressing her.

She kissed him one more time and, reluctantly, made up her mind. "I want to," she said. "But I'm not a pushover."

"I never thought—" Ben protested.

Julie put a finger to his lips to silence him. "Oh, yes, you did," she said. "Come on, let me get up. I'll call you a taxi."

Ben went to the bathroom while she was on the phone. Julie nearly didn't call. Would she ever see him again? She didn't know. But at least, this way, if Ben didn't call, she wouldn't know what she was missing.

And neither would he.

Paul Grace got out of Casualty at two. Neil, despite Paul's protests, had stayed with him. Now he suggested they share a taxi home.

"My car's at the station."

"Are you sure you're in a state to drive, sir?"

"Call me Paul. You're not in my shift now."

"All right … Paul."

"To be honest, Neil, I want to drop by the station, see if anything else has happened."

"To be honest," Neil said, "so do I."

In the taxi, Paul asked Neil a difficult question.

"When you and Clare were going out, did she ever … cheat on you?"

"Not to my knowledge," Neil said. "She's not the type. But a famous footballer can turn some people's heads."

"I don't see what difference it makes."

Neil tried to defend his ex. "Suppose you had a once in a lifetime chance to go to bed with Julia Roberts, just a casual one night stand. Would you turn it down because you were going out with Clare?"

"I don't fancy Julia Roberts," Paul told him. He hated hypothetical questions. Anyway, women never came on to him, not even plain ones. Every woman he'd ever wanted, he had to chase.

"Neither do I, especially," Neil said, "but you take the point."

"I take the point," Paul said. "But I don't accept it. If Clare's spent the night with Umberto Capricio, I'm going to finish with her."

When the Inspector walked into the station there was a round of applause. He tried to look pleased.

"Any progress?" Paul asked.

"None of the team are speaking until they've got lawyers, sir. They all claim it's a case of mistaken identity, even the driver."

"What about the lad I saw there?"

Neil had told Paul about Dean Sutherland being blackmailed by two boys from his past. They didn't yet know which of the two he'd seen in the footballer's house.

"I've got some photographs for you, sir," the sergeant said.

Paul looked at their mugshots.

"That's him."

The sergeant did a PNC check.

"Joseph Hatton. Plenty of form for theft. Last known address a squat in the Meadows. I'll send someone to check if he's returned there. Mother lives in Mansfield. We'll get Mansfield CID to check her place. Known associate: Darren Braithwaite, who has similar form and the same last known address."

"They're also implicated in a suspicious death," Paul told him. "Circulate their photographs, would you?"

"Sir."

The phone rang and Paul, forgetting that this was not his shift, answered it. On the other end was the uniform who'd been guarding Umberto Capricio's house.

"He's just come home, sir."

"Has he? I'll be right over."

Neil Foster stood in the corner of his old Parade room.

"Come on," Paul told him. "Keep me company and I'll give you a lift home afterwards."

"You're on."

In the car, Neil asked, "Are you going to confront him about Clare?"

"I don't know," Paul said. It was the truth, but only just. Inside, he was seething with anger. Catching the motorway team no longer meant anything to him.

"Are you going to tell Umberto about Dean?" Neil asked.

"Not yet. I don't see what purpose it'd serve."

The footballer was sitting in his lounge when they arrived, drinking coffee as though nothing had happened. He stood to offer Paul his hand. Paul ignored him. Neil covered up his rudeness by fussing around the footballer, asking about his mother.

"She slept through it all – unbelievable! They took her jewellery and disconnected her phone. She didn't notice. But she is very deaf. I had to shake her awake when I got in."

"Can you tell me where you were?" Paul asked, in a cold voice.

Umberto gave Clare's address, then turned to Neil.

"Thank you for introducing me to Clare and

174

Gary. I had a very good evening."

"It looked like it," Neil said.

Umberto smiled. "I think the other players were very … envious of me leaving with Clare."

Paul didn't know how what happened next happened. He saw red, that much was certain, and the next thing he knew, he and Capricio were on the floor. Although Umberto was the bigger man, Paul used the advantage of surprise and superior technique. He had the Italian pinned down and began pounding the footballer's face with his fists. As he realized what he was doing, he froze. Umberto tried to shake him off, punching him in the stomach and screaming something in Italian.

"Stop it! Stop it!" Neil shouted, grabbing Paul from behind. "That's enough. Both of you. You'll have the neighbours calling the police again."

Umberto stood, mopping blood from his face. Paul's body ached from where the footballer had hit him. His uniform was all messed up. Umberto turned to Neil.

"What was all that about?" he asked, as though in shock.

"The Inspector is Clare's boyfriend," Neil told him.

To Paul's surprise, Umberto broke into a smile. Paul thought that he was about to say "Not any more, she isn't," but, instead, he held out his arms to give Paul a bear hug.

"So many apologies," Umberto said. "Believe me, I would not have misled you if I had known."

"Misled me," Paul said, as the footballer smothered him for the second time. "You mean you didn't..."

"No. No. Not at all. Please, sit down."

Winded, Paul had little choice but to do as the footballer suggested.

"You can keep a secret?" Umberto asked.

"It's part of the job description."

"I left with Clare and Gary, but Clare was ... what we call in Italy, the Beard. You understand?"

Paul heaved a huge sigh of relief. "You were with Gary."

"I was with Gary."

Now Paul felt like hugging the footballer.

"I'm sorry I—"

"You should not be. Clare is a very beautiful woman. Worth fighting for, I would say."

Paul got up and gave Umberto his hand.

"We'll let you get to bed. An officer will be round tomorrow for a full list of the things that were stolen."

"I have photographs of my mother's jewellery. There's nothing else important. At least they didn't get to the paintings."

"The paintings were what they were after," Paul told him. "If I were you, I'd improve your security."

"If I get any more security, I won't be able to look at them. What is the point of owning paintings that you can't look at?"

"I feel a complete fool," Paul told Neil in the car.

"Better a fool than a cuckold," Neil told him, and he was right, of course. Paul dropped the young DC off, then thought of going to see Clare. It was after three in the morning, but he wanted to wake her, hold her, tell her about his triumph and how much he loved her. But he resisted. He needed some sleep. Later today, Paul had to make sure that the Birmingham task force didn't cock up interviewing the motorway team. Paul also wanted to make sure that the media gave the credit to Notts, rather than DCI Charlton's mob. Paul got home, let himself in, checked the answering machine, then poured himself a malt whiskey, a double, which he took upstairs with him. He sat down on the bed, wishing that Clare was in it. He reached over for his drink, but a wave of tiredness came over him and he fell asleep, fully clothed, without touching it.

16

Melanie brought Neil breakfast in bed. "Thanks for staying," he said.

"It was an eventful evening. I didn't want to miss anything."

Neil recounted the events of the previous evening, only leaving out Umberto's exploits, which he'd promised to be discreet about.

"Is Dean in trouble?" Melanie asked. "He was terribly worried last night."

"He may be charged with aiding and abetting," Neil told her. "The Inspector will send the files to the Crown Prosecution Service. They always make the decision. There are some mitigating factors, but he could get a year inside. Maybe he deserves it."

"He feels terribly guilty."

"I'll bet he does."

"According to him, he went to Umberto's house because he was boxed in, but he was going to tell his mates that a burglary was out of the question. The house was too secure. Then something happened which changed his mind."

"What?"

Melanie hesitated.

"Dean's pretty narrow-minded. I think maybe he misinterpreted what he saw, but, according to him…"

She hesitated. Neil finished the sentence for her.

"He found out that Umberto was gay?"

Melanie nodded. "How did you know? Dean was really embarrassed. I practically had to drag it out of him. He saw some arty photographs. Then, when he was looking for a safe, he came across some pretty explicit magazines hidden away."

"Has he told anyone else?"

"No."

"He'd better keep it that way," Neil said. "He invaded Umberto's privacy. In a way, that's as bad as burgling him."

"Do you think he'll keep his place in the team?"

"I don't know," Neil said. "Maybe, if the story doesn't leak and Umberto's generous, keeps quiet himself. But one thing's for sure."

"What?"

"There's no way that Dean can keep living here."

                              *   *   *

Clare was woken by a phone call from DCI Greasby.

"You're liaison with the task force, so get yourself over to the station asap. Charlton's lot are due in the next hour."

"Why?" Clare said. "What happened?"

"Don't tell me you haven't spoken to your boy-friend yet?"

"Not since yesterday evening."

"Thanks to him, we caught all three of them, last night."

"That's fantastic! I'll be over as soon as I'm dressed."

Jubilant, Clare rang Paul, waking him. "I believe congratulations are in order."

He told her about the previous night, including his fight with Umberto.

"Oh God, how embarrassing! I'm sorry – I didn't see how it would get back to you – I was just trying to help him and Gary out. You say he's got a black eye?"

"Will have, by now," Paul said. "Don't know how he'll explain it to the press, but it should enhance his reputation with the other players."

"Why can't he just…? Oh, never mind. How are you? Did he hurt you?"

"Only a couple of bruises. Look, you'd better get to the station. I don't want Charlton taking all the credit. I'll join you later."

"Why didn't you call the press last night?" Clare asked.

"After last time? Who'd believe me? When we're through with this, can we spend the evening together? There's something I need to talk over with you."

"I'd love to. See you later."

Next, Clare rang her mum, explaining that she couldn't come for Sunday dinner.

"Have you heard from Dad?"

"No. Have you?"

"Not a word. Maybe I should call him at Uncle Angelo's."

"It's up to you. I can't."

Clare felt guilty about missing Mum, and about missing Mass, but it couldn't be helped. She dressed rapidly, deciding to skip breakfast – she'd been gaining weight lately, and wanted to save herself for patisserie in Paris – then knocked on Ruth's door.

"Can I borrow your car? I need to go into work."

Ruth had been in bed for nearly twelve hours, but still looked half-asleep. That couldn't be healthy, Clare thought.

"Are you all right?" she asked.

Ruth grunted, then gave her the keys with a grimace, as though Clare had asked a stupid question. Why did Clare and Paul's triumph have to come at such a rotten time for the people who were closest to her?

*　　*　　*

At the station, the only information the motorway team had divulged was their names. The oldest was Christopher Stevens of Leamington Spa, aged forty-four. The other man who was inside the Capricio house was Timothy Jennings, aged thirty-eight, of Leicester. The driver was Kevin Hunter, forty-two, from Birmingham. None of them had criminal records. All protested their innocence, but refused to say what they were doing by the embankment on Saturday night. They each had lawyers who advised them to give "no comment" interviews. Their failure to speak might count against them in court, but the police had to find the evidence to put them there first.

"Quite a result," DCI Charlton said, when he arrived, half an hour after Clare. He was accompanied by DC Church and DS Cooper from the task force. "Worth missing Sunday dinner with the in-laws for," he added. "Were you in on the arrest?"

"No, sir."

"Just your boyfriend, eh? Where is he?"

"Inspector Grace will be along soon. He had a late night."

Charlton checked the paperwork, what little there was of it.

"Doesn't make sense," he told Clare. "None of this lot has got form, unless you count Broom, and he's in Edinburgh."

"Glasgow," Church corrected him.

"Whatever."

"They're guilty as sin, sir," Clare told the DCI. "Why else would they be there last night? All their lack of a record proves is that they're good criminals."

"How long have you been in CID, Coppola?"

"Not long, sir."

"Then I'll forgive you for thinking that there's such a thing as a *good* criminal. They're all stupid. Some are more stupid than others. And some are luckier than others. But, eventually, it's our turn to get lucky. We only caught this lot because your friend got a lucky break – am I right?"

"I suppose, sir."

Paul would say that you made your own luck. But Clare wasn't going to argue with the egotistical Chief Inspector. Luckily, at that moment, her boyfriend arrived.

"Got a confession yet?" he asked Charlton.

"I've only just arrived. I suppose I ought to congratulate you."

"Thanks."

"I'm presuming that you got the right blokes. I suggest we leave off informing the media until we're ready to charge them. Agreed?"

"Of course," Paul replied. "Provided you can assure me that one of your lot won't leak it."

Charlton frowned, as though this remark was too contemptible to merit an answer.

"I presume you'd like to sit in on the interviews," he said.

They went down to the cells to collect the prisoners.

Joe slept badly, but at least he slept. He wasn't attacked in the night and he wasn't moved along by the police in the morning. He left the cave before the dosser and dog who he'd shared it with began to stir. He walked through the Lace Market, up Fletchergate, then down Bottle Lane into Slab Square, where he used the public toilets to clean himself up. He didn't take a taxi, for the same reason he hadn't taken one the night before – the driver might remember him. Instead, he got on a bus.

Darren wouldn't be there. Even he wasn't stupid enough to go to the most obvious place. Darren would have slept in the car, then taken off somewhere. Stupid sod had no idea where to fence the goods they'd taken. He was probably at a car-boot sale now, trying to flog the jewellery and CDs, getting only a fraction of the pittance a fence would pay (and that was only ten or twenty per cent of the stuff's true value). Joe hoped he got nicked.

The bus driver gave Joe a funny look when he got off at a request stop in what seemed to be the middle of nowhere. Hopefully, he would assume that Joe was a farm labourer. Joe walked back along the busy

A614, which was full of day trippers going to the country parks further along. He took one of the turnings to Blidworth. Joe and Dean used to cycle here when they were kids. It was a decent ride from Mansfield or a short run in a stolen car.

Half a mile down the winding road, Joe reached his destination. The hut was hidden at the back of a copse of trees, in an overgrown corner which didn't seem to belong to anyone. It was too far from a village or town for kids to have adopted it. He couldn't remember now how they'd first found the place. Were they playing hide and seek or had one of them left the narrow road to have a quiet slash? Only once had Joe and Dean found it occupied. A courting couple were using it as a love nest. They'd soon chased them off, bombarding the corrugated iron walls with sticks and stones and clods of earth.

The hut was dilapidated these days, nearly destroyed. Now and then Joe would come with a hammer and nails and whatever he could pick up on the way, try to patch the place up. It still had a roof, but only just. The door had a lock on it, which he'd put there, but anyone who knew could just lift the door off its hinges.

There were no cars in sight. If Darren had been back here, he was gone now. Joe let himself into the hut and looked around the littered floor. There was a faint smell of tobacco. Darren had spent the night here after all. He'd have had some story ready, just in case Joe made it back last night. But Darren was thick. It wouldn't have been a very good story. An empty bottle of vodka was in a corner. Darren would have never got through that on his own. Who the hell was with him?

Joe dug in the space below the hut's one window (though it had no glass, never had, only a square of scratched plastic sheeting). This was the place where he kept his emergency stash of money. He found the stone he kept it under, then scraped around, disbelieving the extent of Darren's betrayal. He'd kill him. The money was gone. All eighty quid. Joe had less than twenty on him.

Then he heard the noise. Footsteps. One set, or two, it was hard to tell. Joe stood, pressing himself into the corner of the hut, ready to leap on Darren if it was him.

It wasn't. A familiar figure stood in the doorway, glaring at him.

"Come out, Joe," Dean Sutherland said.

Joe did as he asked. A young man stepped out from the side of the hut, holding a pair of handcuffs. Joe recognized him. It was Dean's landlord, Neil something, a copper.

"Joseph Hatton," the landlord said, "you're under arrest."

17

"A complete waste of time," DCI Charlton sneered.

You'd think he wasn't pleased that they had captured the three men, Paul thought. But it *was* frustrating, when all you got were endless "no comment" interviews.

"Perhaps," Paul told the Chief Inspector, "we should inform their solicitors that we'll be applying for an extension."

The police had to get permission if they wanted to hold the men for more than twenty-four hours without charging them. An extension lasted only twelve hours and the maximum time they could keep the men without charging them was seventy-two hours. This gave them until just after midnight on Tuesday.

"Won't make any difference," Charlton said. "We need one of them to crack. We need someone to corroborate your identification."

"Candia Arnold might…"

"Fat chance."

Candia Arnold, a supermodel, had seen one of the men's faces. But she was on a shoot in the Bahamas. Her agent thought it unlikely that she would be back in the country before the second week of October.

"Let me have a go at interviewing one of them," Paul said. Charlton hesitated.

"Which one?"

"The driver. He's they guy I saw outside Capricio's without the mask on. He can't deny being there."

"Just one problem," Charlton quibbled.

"What?"

"He didn't do anything, apart from run away. There's nothing to connect him with the others."

"But I saw him with them at the Martin's Arms. That's our ace in the hole. They don't know we have a witness who can put all three of them together."

Charlton seemed unimpressed.

"Maybe a jury will buy the story. But it's your word against the three of them. Juries don't always believe solitary policemen, even if they are Inspectors."

"Give me a go at him."

"All right," Charlton said with a shrug. "Be my guest."

Neil got to the station with Joe Hatton just after one in the afternoon. The lad had cracked, giving a full statement in the car, which Neil would get him to repeat into a tape recorder in the interview room. He had admitted breaking into Umberto Capricio's home. But he denied having seen the two members of the motorway team without their masks on, which was a blow. Neil didn't know if he was telling the truth or not. Maybe a few weeks on remand in a tough nick would change his mind. Joe would be offered a much lighter sentence if he testified against Chris Stevens and Timothy Jennings. His friend, Darren Braithwaite, had no deals to cut if they found him. He would get a heavy sentence – presuming that he was found guilty.

Joe claimed, however, to know nothing about the break-in at Mary Brown's.

"It wasn't me, I swear. Why would I break into my best mate's house?"

"You'd fallen out."

"Not then we hadn't. First I heard was when Darren mentioned she'd had some kind of accident. I didn't even know that she was dead."

"In that case," Neil said, "how do you explain the football?"

Joe looked confused. "What football?"

"The football that was found in the squat where you and Darren were staying."

"Oh, *that* football. I've never actually seen it, but Darren told me he'd left it in the squat. We went and looked for it. Darren said he was looking after the ball for Rob Wardle, until he got out of Glen Parva."

"Rob Wardle?"

"That's right," Joe said. "He's an old mate of Darren's. They were in the same year at school. Rob was coming in to Glen Parva just before I got out. I steered clear of him. He's a hard case. But Darren did a couple of months' stretch with Rob. He said something about holding a signed football that belonged to him, but I never saw it."

Neil put Joe in a cell and went to look for Inspector Grace. He wanted to give him the good news.

"He's carrying out an interview," DC Church told him. "Got anything?"

Neil didn't answer, conscious of how little weight Church had given to Clare's information over the last few weeks. Grace should be the first to know. He walked along to the interview room, outside which DCI Charlton was watching Paul Grace in action.

"Here's what I think happened," the Inspector said to Kevin Hunter. "This was supposed to be the last job. That was why it didn't matter that you were pulling it off near your base in West Bridgford. But you knew the police were on to Eddie, so, just to be on the safe side, you had your planning meeting out in the country rather than at the house, where Eddie was living at the time."

Hunter didn't respond.

"But you needed a base for the raid itself. So, before you assembled there, Eddie did a little decoy run to draw away anyone who was watching the front of the house. No one but Eddie showed themselves at the back, which we were also watching. It worked like a dream, didn't it?"

"My client has no comment," the solicitor said. Paul ignored him.

"Now here's the bit I'm not sure about. Did Christopher Stevens work out that we were about to raid the house or did someone tell him? Because if someone told him when we were watching, and when we got a search warrant, that someone would have to be a police officer, and that information would be very useful to me." He looked straight at the solicitor. "I'd be very grateful and would reward whoever gave me that information. Do I make myself clear?"

"You make yourself very clear, Inspector," the solicitor said.

"So, overnight, you clear out. Like to tell me where?"

"No comment."

"Maybe you just go home. All of you have homes

within an hour, an hour and a half of Nottingham. Except Eddie, who uses the house in West Bridgford. Now Eddie, that night, goes to Glasgow. Which means that the burglary was ready to take place. Why didn't you do it on the Friday night, Kevin? A pity you didn't. Because you'd probably have got away with it. As it was, on Saturday, you ran into an amateur. And I ran into you. I can identify you, Kevin. You were outside that house. And you ran. You'll never be able to explain that to a jury. Your colleagues, they can claim a case of mistaken identity. Probably won't wash, but it might. You gave me some old claptrap about your daughter, who doesn't exist. You're in it up to your neck."

"I didn't even go inside!"

The solicitor hissed into Hunter's ear.

"I wish to have a brief conference with my client."

"Be my guest."

Paul came out.

"Well done," Charlton said. "You nearly had him going there. It's something we can work on."

Paul frowned. He knew that it wasn't enough. Right now, the case relied too heavily on his testimony. But Paul made a good witness in court and had often been complimented on his evidence. He'd make sure they went down.

*   *   *

Neil drove by Umberto's house before going home. A crowd had gathered on the river, watching police frogmen searching for the team's masks and guns, which were presumed to have been thrown into the river. Umberto was watching too.

"Have they found anything?" he asked the Italian.

"A steering wheel, the bones of dead animals, a lot of bottles – no guns, yet. There's a lot of silt in that river. A heavy object like a gun might sink too deep and be impossible to recover. That's what they say."

"We found one of the boys who broke into your house."

"Good. Excellent. Did he have my mother's jewellery?"

"Unfortunately, no," Neil said. "That was the other one. But we'll find him too, in the end. Actually, it was Dean who found the first one."

The footballer's attitude changed from gratitude to suspicion.

"How come?"

"Perhaps we could get a little away from the crowd."

They walked along the riverbank until there was no one within earshot. Neil explained about Dean's criminal past and how he had helped set up the burglary. Umberto shook his head in anger and disbelief.

"Has he told the other players that I'm…"

"No," Neil said. "He won't, I don't think. That's up to you."

Umberto smiled ruefully and stared at the river.

"You can't keep it secret for ever," Neil added.

"Possibly not. But I would prefer it to become public at a time of my choosing." He paused and gave a wry smile. "After I retire, maybe. Footballers can be very – *machismo* – you know what I mean?"

"I know," Neil said. "I'm afraid that Dean won't be able to avoid publicity. It's bound to come out in the next few days. Given that he helped us in the end and that he's agreed to testify against his friend, the Crown Prosecution Service may not press charges. That is, unless you…"

Umberto shook his head.

"What's done is done. Tell Dean I look forward to playing with him on Tuesday."

"I'll tell him."

Neil drove home to give Dean the good news. After he'd told the boy that Umberto was still talking to him, Neil would ask Dean to move out. Umberto might be willing to play with Dean, but Neil wasn't willing to live with him. Police officers couldn't share their homes with criminals, not even unconvicted ones. It was a pity. He'd enjoyed meeting the other footballers and Forest were playing well at the moment. Still, no matter how badly they played, Notts County had always been his team, and always would be.

*   *   *

"So what was it you wanted to ask me?" Clare said, when Paul came back from loading the dishwasher. He sat down on the sofa and put an arm around her.

"It's about how we spend our time in Paris next week."

"You mean, apart from eating in romantic restaurants, taking moonlit walks along the Seine, climbing the Eiffel Tower and…?"

"Yes," Paul said, with a smile, stroking her thigh. "Apart from all that."

"We can do anything you like," Clare told him, with a big smile.

"How about looking for an engagement ring?"

Clare was taken aback. He'd sort of asked her the other night, but, since then, Paul had only hinted that, at some point, they might live together.

"Are you sure about this?" she said. "Are you sure what you're asking me?"

"Yes."

Paul slid off the sofa, on to his knees. He was the second man to do that for her this year.

"Clare, I love you. I've never felt this way about anybody before. I want to spend the rest of my life with you. Will you marry me?"

18

Ruth's transfer came through on Tuesday. Opening the letter, she felt relieved and sure that she'd made the right decision. But her mood changed as she read to the bottom of the page. It was an insult. They wanted to send her to the one place where they knew she couldn't go.

When Ruth got home after her early shift, Clare was still in. Her friend was on a three-to-eleven. Ruth told her what had happened.

"Do they *know*?" Clare asked.

"They know I'm going out with someone in that shift. I'm always getting teased about it. They don't know that I've split up with him."

"So you're going to turn it down, right?"

"I don't know," Ruth said. "I don't know how

long I can stand it where I am."

"Then maybe you should do it," Clare told her. "After all, being on the same shift as Ben might be a good way to get over him … or get back together."

"We won't be getting back together," Ruth said.

"Are you sure?"

"I'm sure," she said.

"Remember at Ryton," Clare said, "how we used to hope that we'd end up on the same shift together?"

"And now I might be replacing you."

"You'd be working with Gary," Clare pointed out. "You'd like that."

"But he's Ben's partner."

"That's OK. You and Gary share a house. You wouldn't want to be partners as well."

"If he was straight I might," Ruth commented, and both women laughed.

"That's the first joke I've heard you make since it happened," Clare said. "Go on, do it. Give Paul a ring."

Clare was bullying her into making a decision, but Ruth didn't mind. Friends were allowed to bully each other for their own good. Was this going to be good? A flicker of doubt crossed Ruth's mind.

"He's not taking me on as a favour to you, is he?" she asked Clare.

"He hasn't even mentioned it to me," Clare said. She picked up the phone, dialled the number and asked for Inspector Grace. Then she passed the phone to Ruth.

"I'm still not sure," Ruth mumbled, as Paul Grace's voice came through the ear piece.

"Ruth? Is that you?"

"Hi," she said, reluctantly holding the receiver.

"I've just been given notification that you might be joining us."

"Me too," Ruth said. So he hadn't known. "How do you feel about it?"

"Great," Paul said, with gusto. "There's just one thing. Clare told me you and Ben are over. Is that still the case?"

"Yes," Ruth said. "I wouldn't think of coming if it wasn't."

"There's no chance…?"

"No," Ruth asserted, "absolutely none."

"All right. Well, you're both professionals – I'm sure it won't get in the way of your working together. I'll break it to him gently."

"You do that," Ruth said.

"See you in a fortnight."

"I'm looking forward to it."

She put the phone down.

"You're in?" Clare asked.

"I'm in!"

The two women hugged, then Ruth burst into hysterical giggles.

"What is it?" Clare asked.

Ruth smiled wryly. "What I wouldn't give to see the look on Ben's face when he finds out."

That evening, Paul was called in to provide extra cover for the cup tie against County. He wasn't a big football follower, but enjoyed public order work. A big cup tie was a high stakes event, where the officer in command proved himself – or not. After nabbing the motorway team, Paul wasn't afraid of failure.

The three men still hadn't been charged. It was frustrating. Charlton claimed that he was trying to get Candia Arnold back from the Bahamas and trace Eddie Broom. Phil Church had been sent to Glasgow to question him. Still, with Paul as an eye witness, the Crown Prosecution Service had enough evidence to put the other three away. Charlton had promised that they would be charged today, before the deadline expired at midnight.

The County fans, expecting to lose, were good natured, especially when their side took a surprise early lead and hung on to it. Forest were having trouble. From what little Paul could gather of the game, Umberto Capricio was carrying an injury, as well as a black eye (the local press were having lots of fun speculating about that one). Just before the end of the second half, a Forest midfielder was substituted, and young Dean Sutherland came on. Within seconds, he was making a long run from deep in his own half, taking the ball past two defenders, running straight at goal.

Dean didn't hesitate. He had a good chance of a shot but the angle was tight. The young player must have seen Capricio slip his marker, for he dummied a defender and the goalie into thinking that he was going to shoot, then laid on the ball for Umberto. The goalkeeper was already committed to diving in the other direction. Umberto had an open goal. Even Paul, who didn't play football, wouldn't have missed it. Umberto put the ball into the bottom left hand corner of the goal, but he wasn't quick enough. A County defender threw himself across the goal line and cleared it. The full time whistle blew before Forest could take their corner. The scores were level on aggregate.

Extra time was uneventful. Both teams seemed unwilling to take risks. There were no replays in two-legged games. If the game stayed a draw, it would go to a penalty shoot out.

Paul thought about Clare as he scanned the monitors, looking for trouble. On Sunday night, he had asked her to marry him. He'd been as sure as he'd ever been sure of anything that she would say "yes". They were in love. He couldn't imagine them being any more in love. But Clare had become upset. Her parents' separation had hit her harder than Paul realized. Suddenly, she said, marriage didn't seem like the be all and end all of love. Instead, it seemed like a huge risk. So, thanks, but no thanks.

Paul had told her he understood, but still hoped she'd change her mind. She loved him, that was the important thing. Clare wasn't fickle, and neither was he. So Paul still day-dreamed of a spring wedding. On Friday, they would fly to Paris, where they could choose a ring, if Clare did come round to the idea.

It wasn't just Clare's parents, Paul knew. Clare was also affected by Ben and Ruth splitting up. No one had seen that coming, except, maybe, for Ben himself. Thinking of those two reminded Paul that he hadn't told Ben Shipman the news about Ruth yet. He would be annoyed, Paul guessed, but that was his problem. Paul had read his new recruit's file. Ruth was a reliable copper: not headstrong, like Clare, or ambitious, like her ex-boyfriend, but sound. She was just what the shift needed.

Paul's thoughts were interrupted when he spotted someone on the monitor. He must be imagining it. But it certainly looked like him. Paul radioed one of the officers on the ground and asked him to get Neil Foster, bring him to the control room. Neil arrived a minute later.

"Sir, I'm not on duty and the penalty shoot out's going to start any minute. Can't whatever it is wait?"

"Your team are doing better than expected," Paul commented.

"Yes," Neil said, impatiently, "that's why—"

"I only need you to make an identification, Neil. Look." He pointed out the man on the screen.

Neil smiled. "Darren Braithwaite. Well-spotted, sir. This is quite a week you're having."

Paul grinned. He radioed a message for Braithwaite to be arrested.

"I like to tie up loose ends before I go off on holiday."

Neil was obviously itching to get back to the game, but he stopped at the door.

"I hope you and Clare have a great time in Paris. You both deserve one."

"Thanks, Neil. I appreciate you saying that."

With a large smile on his face, Paul went down to the holding cells to deal with Braithwaite. The final whistle went.

The score was one-all on aggregate, so it went to penalties. Dean didn't know whether to volunteer or not. He'd never taken a penalty for Forest. He'd only had a couple for the reserves at Mansfield, but had put both of them away.

No need to worry. The manager had his five already picked. Thankfully, they were all still on the pitch.

"And I'd like volunteers for numbers six and seven," he said, "just in case."

Suddenly, everybody else was looking at the ground.

"Come on," the manager said. "It'll probably never happen."

It was bound to come out in the papers, Neil had

told Dean. He could do with some glory to offset the scandal that was about to overtake his career.

"All right," he said, in a strangled voice. "I'll do number six, if it comes to it."

"Good lad," the manager said. "Now, who'll be number seven?"

"Where do you think you're taking him?" asked the bloke who was sitting with Darren Braithwaite. He was ugly and built like a tank, with a dirty pencil moustache. On the pitch, County scored a penalty, making it 2-1.

"None of your business," Paul said.

"Leave him alone. He's done nothing."

Forest equalized.

"It's the penalty shoot out!" Darren complained, as County put another away. "Can't it wait, just a minute?"

Paul cautioned him. Some of the other spectators began to complain about the disturbance. The big bloke threatened one of them with his fists.

"Better bring him in, too," Paul told the uniform accompanying him.

"Tell me," Paul said, as the men were led to the holding cells. "What were you two doing the Saturday before last?"

"Don't remember," Darren said, as Forest equalized again.

"No use asking me," the other one said. "I only

got out of Glen Parva on Friday. Look, can't you hold on and let us watch this? There's only two more penalties each."

"Tough," Paul said, pushing them inside. "I'll tell you what – give me everything I want to know, and I'll let you know the score afterwards."

The crowd went deathly quiet as County took their fourth penalty. The Forest keeper made a brilliant save and the home crowd erupted. Still 3-3. Paul slammed the door shut.

"What's your name?" he asked the big one.

"Wardle. Robert Wardle."

"Perhaps you'd like to account for your movements on Saturday night, Robert. Take a moment to think about it, though. I've got a phonecall to make."

While the two lads sweated it out, Paul rang Glen Parva.

"I want to find out about a lad you've just released. Name of Wardle…"

Neil held his breath as Forest took their fourth penalty. He couldn't believe that County had got this close. It would all be over in a minute. The Forest captain shot for the bottom right-hand corner of the goal. Somehow, the County keeper got a hand to it. The ball hit the goalpost, then bounced back. Neil was sure that it was going to go in but the ball kept just ahead of the goal line. The County keeper kicked it away. Neil cheered himself hoarse. They were still even.

County made no mistake with their fifth penalty and then Forest equalized. 4-4.

So it was sudden death. As soon as one team scored, and the other missed, the game would be over and the winners would be through to the third round. The County players seemed to be arguing among themselves over who should take their sixth penalty. Neil groaned. None of them wanted the responsibility for losing, a bad sign. The end was nigh. To Neil's surprise, the goalie came forward. He did a short run up and hit the ball directly at the Forest keeper.

The Forest keeper, however, made his move before the other keeper had kicked the ball. He dived to the right. If he'd stayed still, he would have saved it. As it was, County were ahead 5-4. Who would take the next Forest penalty? As Neil expected, Forest had it all planned out. But he couldn't believe the identity of the player stepping nervously forward. It was Dean Sutherland.

"Not with your boyfriend tonight?" Dad asked Clare on the phone. It was the first time they'd spoken in the eight days since she'd heard they were splitting up. She'd tried to get hold of him, but he'd been out, doing long hours on site, according to Clare's aunt.

"No. Paul's working. But we're going away next weekend. Paris."

"Sounds nice. Sounds like you're pretty serious about each other, too."

"Yes," Clare said. "I guess we are." She was feeling a bit guilty about turning Paul down. A bit foolish, too. She should have asked for time to think about it, as she had when Neil asked her. Paul seemed to understand why she refused him, but, even so, he was bound to have been hurt.

"I'm glad you're happy with someone. You know, *tesore*, your mother and I didn't want to tell you what was happening until you had someone … close, you understand?"

"I understand," Clare said.

"But the way you've been these last few weeks, we both said we've never seen you so happy."

"I love him very much," Clare told her father, surprising herself, because they didn't usually talk this way.

"So don't let our problems spoil your happiness. Promise me."

"I promise," Clare said. "At least, I'll try."

"That's my girl. How's Maria?"

"Mum's fine. She's making your bedroom into a living-room." Clare thought for a moment that she shouldn't have told Dad this, but he laughed.

"Varnishing the floor, huh? She always wanted to do that."

"How are you getting on with Uncle Angelo?" Clare asked.

Dad was silent for a moment. "It's not easy," he said, eventually. "A man of forty-nine working for his older brother. I've had to learn some … humility. But maybe it's not a bad thing. Angelo's looking after me very well, keeping me busy."

"I want to see you soon," Clare said.

"Give things time to settle down," Dad told her. "There's plenty of time. And give my love to Maria."

"I will," Clare said. She hung up the phone and began to make a decision.

Umberto Capricio patted Dean on the shoulder.

"Hard luck. It was a lot of pressure for your first cup tie."

Dean found himself crying. He was grateful to Capricio, but he'd never get over missing that penalty. Dean couldn't believe now that he'd actually volunteered to take the sixth penalty. He remembered stepping forward. He remembered choosing his spot. He remembered the desperate rumble of the crowd. What he didn't remember was how he'd managed to blast the ball way above the goal, into the stand.

The players were all friendly, sympathetic. They invited him along for a drink afterwards. But Dean decided to slink off home. Not that he had a home to go to.

On the way out, Neil was waiting for him.

"Would you mind coming with me?"

This was it, Dean thought. He was about to be arrested for setting up Capricio. Neil had warned that it might be out of his hands, that the DPP might decide to make an example of him, no matter what facts the police put in mitigation. He asked why Neil was taking him to the station.

"There's someone I want you to see," Neil said, suppressing a huge smile. Of course, he was a County supporter. "Bad luck about the penalty, by the way," Neil added. "Could have happened to anyone."

Neil took him down to the holding cells. There was Darren Braithwaite, looking lost. In the next cell was someone Dean remembered.

"You recognized him?" Neil asked, after taking Dean back upstairs.

"Yeah. Rob Wardle. Used to go to my school. He's a real psycho."

"It seems that this real psycho was the one responsible for Mary's death."

"What? I thought that Joe and Darren…"

Neil shook his head. "Joe had nothing to do with it. Unless you count him getting Darren to follow you home from the pub one night in order to find out where you live. It was Rob's bright idea to rob you. He was on home-leave the weekend before he was released. Darren went along with it. Joe didn't know. He was at the Sheffield Wednesday game, watching you play. In fact, the whole Capricio burglary was Rob's idea, too. Darren talked Joe into blackmailing you."

"I don't under—"

"Rob and Darren ripped off Joe that night. All along, they'd planned to take the money and run."

"Poor Joe," Dean said, wrapped up in his thoughts. He added, out of politeness, "You did well, working it all out."

"It was all down to Inspector Grace," Neil said. "I just helped out a little."

Neil drove Dean home. "Don't take too long finding somewhere new to live," he said.

Dean nodded. He could get a flat with Joe, he thought. Joe was his only real friend, and had nowhere to go. Joe hadn't betrayed him, at least not until Dean let him down first. Maybe they could make it up. But then he remembered that Joe was still in the nick for burgling Umberto. And, the police had warned, there would be publicity. Instead of looking for a new home, Dean might be looking for a transfer. But where? Even abroad, the story was bound to follow him. The player who had one of his teammates burgled. His career could be over before it had begun.

There was surprisingly little trouble after the match, so Paul got home by twenty-past ten. It had been a satisfying day, getting those two burglars on top of everything else. They'd coughed to the Mary Brown burglary, and explained how she died. Paul wasn't sure whether a manslaughter charge would stick, but it was still an excellent and unexpected result.

Paul meant to call Clare as soon as he got inside, the way he did every night when they weren't together. If she wasn't too tired, he might suggest that she come over. He'd give her a lift to work in the morning. Paul wanted to tell her about Darren Braithwaite and Rob Wardle. It was great, he reflected as he parked, having someone who understood, someone to share things with.

Come to think of it, he would give Birmingham a ring before he called Clare, make sure they'd charged the three men from the motorway team. Then it could be a double celebration. Tomorrow, he'd be fielding press interviews right, left and centre.

As Paul activated the alarm on his car, a heavy shadow fell across him. A dark blue van pulled up right outside his house, blocking out the light from the street lamps. Paul looked around. The first thing he noticed was that the van's front number-plate was missing. He tried to see who was inside the vehicle, but its windows were too dark and dirty. Then the side door slid back. Paul recognized the driver, who was pointing a sawn-off shotgun at him.

Before Paul could react, the driver fired the shotgun, deafening him. There was no time to feel fear, or pain. Paul was thrown back against the front door of his home.

He was dead before his body hit the ground.

EPILOGUE

It was well after eleven. Ruth and Sam were both in bed, unaware why Clare was acting so excitedly. Clare would have liked to share her good news with both of them, but wanted to choose her moment carefully. Maybe Ruth would have picked herself up by the time that Clare came back from Paris, next Monday, wearing her new engagement ring.

Because, since talking to her father, Clare had decided that she would marry Paul after all. She meant to go over tonight and tell him, no matter what time he got home. The thing was, Mum and Dad's break-up had hit her hard, but it wasn't a reason to back away from marriage. Maybe, Clare had worked out, her getting married would be a way of pressing Mum and Dad to spend time with each other again. Maybe it would even bring them back together for good. You never knew what was going to happen.

Clare kept thinking of new things. When would she and Paul get married? And where? There was so much stuff that they'd hardly discussed. Religion, for instance. Dad would go ballistic if they didn't wed in a Catholic church. But Paul might have his own church, or prefer a registry office. Clare, given the choice, would like to marry in the city's Roman Catholic cathedral. She'd broach the subject with him once they were in Paris.

Clare was tired, but waited patiently for Paul to ring. Tonight's match had gone to extra time and penalties and the home side had lost. There was bound to have been trouble after the game. That would be why he was so late.

"Newsnight" finished. Clare turned the TV off, then looked out of the window at the people on the street, who were slowly drifting away from the pub. She had never been happier than she was now. The other loves in her life paled into insignificance beside Paul. Maybe they shouldn't wait for the wedding, but move in with each other straight away. It seemed crazy to ever spend another night apart.

A police car pulled up in front of the house and two officers got out of it: a man and a woman. In the dark, Clare couldn't tell who they were. She wondered what they wanted. Most people, seeing this sight at their door late at night, would be worried. Clare wasn't. The house was always getting calls from other officers.

The doorbell rang. Without a care in the world, Clare went to answer it.

What happens next? Read

NIGHTSHIFT

and find out...

The car entered a wide driveway, parked out of sight from the street. The driver turned to Joe. "Got something for you in the garage."

Joe followed him. It didn't feel right, though. The garage light went on.

"This wasn't to get Loscoe out," Joe told the driver, sensing the other one coming up behind. "This was to get me."

"Correct," said a third man, stepping out of the shadows. Joe knew his name: Christopher Stevens. He was the motorway team's leader. And he was holding a gun.

"I'd never have testified against you," Joe said. "You've got to believe me, I..."

"We don't believe in taking risks," Stevens said, pointing the gun at him. "You were in the wrong place at the wrong time, Sunny Jim. You're dead."